A
Harlequin
Romance

OTHER
Harlequin Romances
by REBECCA STRATTON

Many of these titles are available at your local bookseller,
or through the Harlequin Reader Service.

For a free catalogue listing all available Harlequin Romances,
send your name and address to:

HARLEQUIN READER SERVICE,
M.P.O. Box 707, Niagara Falls, N.Y. 14302
Canadian address: Stratford, Ontario, Canada   N5A 6W4

or use the coupon at the back of this book.

MOON TIDE

by

REBECCA STRATTON

Harlequin Books

TORONTO • LONDON • NEW YORK • AMSTERDAM • SYDNEY • WINNIPEG

Original hard cover edition published in 1975
by Mills & Boon Limited

SBN 373-01955-6

Harlequin edition published March 1976

Printed in Canada

CHAPTER ONE

KATE was tired, but the churning sense of excitement she felt at actually arriving at last did a lot to compensate for nine thousand miles of flying, from London to Honolulu in one day, and she took her first look at the Hawaiian islands with bright, expectant eyes. Honolulu Airport, of course, was much like any other airport in a lot of ways, but it was bright and bustling and colourful, and it fitted in with her own eager mood of anticipation perfectly.

The very size of the airport complex left her gasping when she thought of London's strictly functional airport and when she compared them the contrast could hardly have been more complete. There seemed to be flowers everywhere, and everyone seemed to be draped in at least one of the famous and traditional *leis*, those garlands of welcome made from blossoms of every colour and so heavily fragrant that the air was quite heady with it.

Kate found it all very exciting, but confusing too, for the number and variety of races pouring in and out of the terminal building was as varied and colourful as the flowers in their *leis*, and she had no idea where to go or who to ask directions of.

Having successfully passed through the requisite check points she then found herself heading, via an incredible display of Oriental and Polynesian gardens, for the outside world, the road to Honolulu itself, and there she would be completely lost. She had reached the point when she simply had to ask someone when a brown-skinned man in uniform spotted her and smiled as if he guessed her predicament.

'You looking for somewhere, ma'am?' he asked, and for the first time it really came home to Kate that this particular Pacific paradise was as much a part of the United States of America as New York or Texas.

Any assistance was welcome at the moment and that of a man in uniform in particular, and she smiled in return, a small and rather uncertain smile as she stood down her cases for a moment. 'I have to get to Borka Point,' she explained. 'Is it very far?'

The man's cheerful face broke into a grin, and he looked down at her diminutive figure and the two suitcases standing beside her. 'Well, it's a whole lot too far to walk, honey, that's for sure,' he told her. 'Look now, you just keep right on walking the way you are and pretty soon you'll find plenty of cabs waiting. O.K.?'

Kate picked up her suitcases again, the first obstacle overcome. 'Thank you,' she said. 'Thank you very much!'

Her informant raised a hand in a gesture that was neither salute nor wave but a combination of both, and he grinned good-naturedly. '*Aloha!*' he said cheerfully.

His prophecy that there would be plenty of cabs available proved to be quite true, and Kate had no trouble at all finding one willing to take her to Borka Point. The driver was a young and cheerful Hawaiian of mixed blood, whose slightly tilted eyes suggested a touch of the Oriental, and he cheerfully heaved her luggage into the taxi, assuring her that he knew the address she asked for well.

Her own looks were attractive enough to draw a second look even in these islands of quite incredibly attractive people, and she had not missed the appreciative and quite frankly approving gleam in the eyes of the taxi driver. She had a small nose that was inclined to turn up slightly at its tip, and a mouth that was just a little too wide, but full and soft enough to be completely feminine.

Wide green eyes were fringed with thick brown lashes the same colour as her nut-brown hair and set in a small, oval and deceptively childlike face, and her figure, while small enough to be called petite, was softly rounded and did a lot to the simple linen dress she wore.

'You stayin' long time?' the driver enquired suddenly, and Kate smiled a little uncertainly. She was not used to having taxi drivers take an interest in her plans, but then she had never been in the Hawaiian islands before.

'It rather depends,' she told him cautiously. 'I'm not really sure yet.'

'Yeah?' The tilted eyes gleamed with friendly curiosity and he smiled at her via the rear mirror which was angled so as to see his passengers rather than to give him a view of the road behind. 'You English?' he asked, and beamed his pleasure at being right when Kate nodded her head.

'Yes, I am,' she said. 'I left London only this morning.'

'Plenty long flight!' the driver remarked, and again treated her to a long and frankly curious scrutiny. 'You belong ole man Wilmot?'

His pronunciation of her own and her great-uncle's surname left her staring blankly for a moment, but then she realised what he had said and immediately frowned over the familiarity, not to mention the disrespect, implied by the question. 'Mr. Charles Wilmot was my uncle,' she informed him, leaving no doubt how she felt about his attitude. 'I'm here for the reading of his will.'

'Good fella!'

The spontaneous opinion overcame her natural reticence after a moment or two, and she realised that this cheerful, brown-faced little Hawaiian probably knew far more about her Uncle Charles Wilmot than she did herself. 'Did you—did you know Mr. Wilmot?' she asked, and the driver nodded, giving her another broad smile via the rear-view mirror.

'Sure!' he said. 'Good fella! He an' paintin' fella, both good fellas!'

Whoever the painting fella was he did not interest Kate, but she counted herself lucky to have come across someone so soon who had actually known her uncle, and what was more, apparently admired him. 'He used to hire your taxi?' she asked, and the driver again nodded and grinned.

'Plenty times!' he assured her, and chuckled richly. 'He good-time fella!' A broad wink conveyed much more than the actual words did and

Kate hastily avoided that meaningful gaze in the mirror.

It would probably have been easy enough to discover exactly what it was he was hinting at, but she had no desire to delve into anything about her uncle that was likely to prove embarrassing, so instead she said nothing. Whatever Charles Wilmot had been or done, he was dead now, and sleeping dogs should be allowed to lie.

Preoccupation made her uncommunicative and the driver may have taken her quietness for a snub, but whatever his reasons, he ceased his enquiries long enough for her to have time to think. In fact, Charles Wilmot had been her great-uncle, her Grandfather Wilmot's older brother, and she had known very little about him, except a few sparse and barely credible tales passed on by her father who had never seen him in person.

Charles Wilmot had been wealthy when he died at eighty-four years old, that much she knew about him, and he had eventually settled down as the owner of a thriving business after years of roaming around the world, but so little had been said about him that Kate always suspected he might have led a rather less than respectable life before he became a property owner.

He had never married, so far as any of the family knew, and Kate had heard rumours and hints at various times that suggested he might have been in love with her paternal grandmother. Certainly his wanderings seemed to have commenced about the time she married his younger brother, but she had never heard the story confirmed, and questions about him were not encouraged.

He had been in the South Seas ever since his early thirties and had settled in Oahu, the busiest and most commercial of the Hawaiian islands, long before it became part of the fiftieth state of America. For some years spasmodic letters had been exchanged, but these had gradually dwindled off and finally ceased altogether. The news of Kate's birth, twenty-two years ago, must have been almost the last news to arrive before communications broke down completely.

Kate had often wished she knew more about her mysterious great-uncle, and more especially since she had learned of his death a couple of months ago and learned, like a bolt out of the blue, that she was one of his heirs. He must have been an interesting and colourful character, and it was not hard to understand why the letters had eventually ceased, for he could have had little in common with the rest of his rather conservative family.

She still found it incredibly hard to believe that she actually owned property in this exotic and almost unbelievable part of the world. Exactly what her inheritance consisted of she had yet to learn in full, but she was to go straight to the house her uncle owned, so that at least must be a part of it. Who or what the old man's other heirs were, she had no idea yet, and that was what gave her her only niggle of doubt.

The journey out to Borka Point proved as interesting and exciting as she expected, although she was a little disappointed that she could not actually see the famous Waikiki beach as they passed it.

High rise hotels and wealthy yacht clubs hid it from her view for the most part, and it was only later on, when they got into the Diamond Head area that she was able to fully appreciate the breathtaking splendours of the Hawaiian scenery.

The sea was far below, bright and sparkling blue under a blue sky, rolling on to sandy beaches and in other places crashing on to the rocks at the foot of soaring cliffs with only the roof-tops of the luxurious, sea-facing homes showing below among their surrounding trees.

The drive seemed to go on for so long that Kate began to think her destination must lie on the far side of the island, but then suddenly the taxi took a sharp right turn and headed along a steep, shrub-lined road towards the sea. The descent was breathtaking and she clung to the side of the seat as they swept round on to a neat gravelled drive.

'Borka Point,' the driver informed her with a grin. 'Down here is Hale Makai!'

His pronunciation of the name of her uncle's house was quite different from the one she had given it, and she frowned for a moment, trying to commit it to memory. If she could at least pronounce the name of her newly acquired property correctly, it might serve to impress Mr. Robert Chang, her uncle's attorney.

Kate was not entirely sure why she should think so, but she could not rid herself of the idea that there would be certain objections to her taking possession of the house. Mr. Chang's letters to her had been polite and formal and couched in correct legal terms, but somehow she could not get the idea

11

out of her head that he did not altogether approve of some unknown English girl coming out to claim island property.

She had barely time to shake her head impatiently over her own imaginative ramblings when there it was in front of her suddenly, at the end of a long winding drive, crowded round with the most brilliant and beautiful collection of flowing shrubs and trees she could ever have imagined.

It was like a dream suddenly come true. The big white sprawling two-storey house with a balcony running the whole width of it and disappearing round one end, and a flight of steps giving access to the balcony. One side of it, she realised, must actually overhang the ocean, and the thought of what that view must be like was breathtaking.

The driveway ended in a kind of forecourt where a fountain splashed gently into a wide stone basin containing red and pink waterlilies. The whole setting was so much like something out of a television film set that Kate shook her head in disbelief.

So far there seemed to be no one else about and Kate's heart was thudding in wild panic suddenly as she faced the unknown. Until the taxi driver spoke there was no other sound to be heard but the soft splashing of the water in the fountain and the distant, less gentle voice of the surf below on the beach.

'You shout, somebody come!' the driver advised cheerfully, and called out something that was quite unintelligible to her before pocketing his fare and climbing once more into his cab. 'Somebody come!' he assured her with another grin, and waved a cheerful hand as he drove off.

Standing alone on the paved forecourt Kate had never felt so deserted or so nervous in her life before, and she was bitterly disappointed at the lack of hospitality, when she had expected so much of the famous Hawaiian welcome. Surely, even if no one had heard the taxi arrive, they must have heard the driver's shout, but the house stood as quiet and unresponsive as ever, and she shrugged at last and walked across to what appeared to be the only way into the house apart from the balcony steps.

Leaving her suitcases, she wandered across, her heart hammering wildly and a strange curling sense of expectation in her stomach. The scent of the flowers was almost overpowering, and she thought for a brief moment of her own very English little garden back home.

The perfume of roses, woodbine and night-scented stock was sweet enough on a summer night, but the overpowering sweetness and variety of these blossoms was incredible. Impulsively she broke off a big, fragrant pink blossom from its tree and held it to her nose, inhaling its perfume, and she was so preoccupied that she gave a cry of alarm when someone spoke from behind her.

'Kate Wilmot?'

She spun round swiftly, her eyes wide and startled, and the blossom fell from her fingers on to the ground. Heaven knew where he had come from, certainly not from the house or from the balcony steps, or she would have seen him, but she found herself face to face with a man who regarded her with eyes as dark as the little taxi driver's had been, but there was something else beside friendly curiosity in this man's gaze.

It was bold and speculative and it aroused in her an immediate resentment that was due in part, she had to admit, to his familiar use of her name. He was much taller than the taxi driver too, but he could have been Hawaiian, his skin was such a glowing, golden bronze and his hair so jet black.

Yet there was a look about his features that was more European, despite his colouring. A strong, square jaw and a wide firm mouth, slightly crooked at one corner and with deep creases that suggested he laughed a lot. He regarded her down the impressive length of a strong, hawkish nose in contrast to which long black lashes looked positively feminine.

He wore a pair of thin cotton trousers that might once have been white or cream, but were now splashed and stained with streaks of vari-coloured paints. He wore no shirt and nothing on his feet, and he looked just about as disreputable as it was possible to look, so that Kate viewed with disfavour the idea of finding him on her doorstep.

Something in her brain groped for recognition and she remembered suddenly the taxi driver's reference to a 'paintin' fella', coupled in the same compliment as her uncle. Who he was or where he had come from she had no idea, but she hoped he was not to be her sole welcomer. He looked so perfectly at home standing there on the forecourt with his head cocked to one side enquiringly that Kate frowned.

'I'm looking for a Mrs. Leith,' she told him in what she hoped was a discouraging voice, and he inclined his head in the direction of the open door.

'Have you tried going in?' he asked, and Kate shook her head.

She was reluctant to admit that sheer nervousness had kept her from walking straight in and taking possession of her property and she suspected he knew it from the deep, unholy gleam in the watching eyes. Everything was so new and strange to her, and she was not even sure who Mrs. Leith would prove to be, only that Mr. Chang had said she would be there to meet her when she arrived.

'I—I didn't like to just walk in,' she admitted, and immediately regretted the hint of apology in her voice.

One black brow elevated into a thick swathe of hair over his forehead, and he quirked that crooked mouth into a smile. 'Scared?' he enquired, and before Kate could deny it he slipped a hand under her elbow with easy familiarity and propelled her towards the door.

'My cases!' She half turned in his grasp to go back for her luggage, but he forestalled her, letting go her arm and picking up the cases with an ease that made her blink.

'Leith must be around somewhere,' he told her as he again guided her into the house. 'But you're perfectly entitled to walk into your own house without waiting for the housekeeper to admit you!'

'Oh!' She turned her head and looked at him

uncertainly. Mr. Chang had said nothing about Mrs. Leith being a housekeeper, but it was a comforting thought, for at least it meant there would be someone to take care of things until she got used to them herself.

'Didn't you know that?' her companion asked, and laughed shortly without giving her time to answer. He steered her through the big doorway and into a cool and spacious hall that was as deserted as the outside had been. The fingers that curled about her arm were as strong as steel and she would have liked to shake herself free of them, but at the moment she was grateful for his help, even if it was only until the tardy Mrs. Leith put in an appearance.

He dumped both her cases down and looked around, then raised his voice. 'Mrs. Leith! Mrs. Leith, our lady's arrived!'

The housekeeper must have been somewhere in the back of the house, for she came into the hall in answer to his call from a door at the back of the hall, a tall, thin-faced woman with grey hair and narrow grey eyes, and with no trace of the usual mixed racial colouring Kate had seen in almost everyone so far.

She disapproved of being called, that much was obvious from the tightness of her mouth, and Kate's heart sank at the sight of her. This would be no friendly, helpful housekeeper who would try and make things easier for her. It was quite evident from her expression that Mrs. Leith was not pleased to see her new employer.

'Miss Wilmot's arrived,' Kate's companion told

16

her, rather superfluously in the circumstances. 'Take charge of her, will you, Mrs. Leith?'

The thin body of the housekeeper pulled itself up, tautly resentful. 'Of course, Mr. Fernandez,' she said in a chillingly cool voice. 'That's what I'm here for!' She looked down at the two suitcases standing beside Kate and raised one brow. 'That's all your luggage, Miss Wilmot?' she asked, and Kate nodded, feeling suddenly like a poor relation.

'That's all,' she said, and before she could add anything more by way of explanation, the man beside her laughed shortly.

'You don't have to apologise to Mrs. Leith for not having a Hollywood style wardrobe,' he told her, his dark eyes glittering. 'No one needs much in the way of clothes here.'

'Oh, I intend buying more when I've learned my way around,' Kate told him hastily, not altogether happy about his defence of her. 'I simply didn't bother bringing much with me.'

'Oh, I see.' He was leaning against the elaborate balustrade at the foot of the stairs and he regarded her for a moment with a gaze that was partly curious and wholly amused. 'Being old Charlie's heir isn't going to change your life-style, then?' he suggested, and laughed again. 'Lucky girl!'

Kate felt the flush of colour that warmed her cheeks and decided that whoever he was, the 'paintin' fella' was not going to be a welcome visitor at Hale Makai. She drew herself up to her full five feet one inch and tried to appear as she imagined an heiress should appear when she had just taken possession of her inheritance.

'I'm very grateful to you for helping me, Mr.— Fernandez?' she told him, 'but I can manage now, thank you, I needn't trouble you any further.' She proffered a hand and he smiled.

Instead of immediately shaking her hand and taking his leave however, he merely looked at it for a moment, then engulfed it in his own massive one and squeezed so hard she winced. 'I'm Kai Fernandez, Miss Wilmot,' he told her in a quiet and quite serious voice, 'but I'm afraid you can't dismiss me quite as easily as you seem to think!' He seemed to find her obvious bewilderment amusing, for his eyes glittered with it. 'You see,' he added softly, 'I'm also one of the heirs, and Hale Makai belongs as much to me as it does to you!'

Kate had never had such a shock in her life and she still could scarcely believe that she was expected to share her uncle's house with a stranger. She had known from the outset that there were other heirs to the estate, but she had expected to have the house to herself and she faced the prospect of sharing it with a man like Kai Fernandez with something akin to despair.

The situation was impossible, of course, she could not share the same house as a strange man and one of them would have to go. Since she was Charles Wilmot's great-niece the one to go would have to be the stranger to the family, and she would tell him so as soon as she had recovered a little from her long journey.

Her room was quite the most beautiful room she had ever seen, and she had said as much to the straight-faced Mrs. Leith, but her enthusiasm had brought little more than a slight lifting of one brow and a curious gesture with that tight mouth that could have meant anything, most likely disapproval.

A huge wooden bed, with neither head nor footboard, stood where it was possible to see the ocean from its comfort, and daintly frilled bed covers suggested either that Charles Wilmot had entertained female company, or that the room had been prepared especially for her, and in view of her reception she was more inclined to believe the former most likely.

From the window she could see literally for miles, and yet the house was private and nestled into its own little jungle of exotic trees and shrubs above the golden sanded beach. It would have been wonderful to own such a house had it been hers alone, but to have to share it—— She frowned yet again at her reflection in the long dressing mirror and shrugged helplessly. Until she knew more about the contents and conditions of the will there was nothing she could do.

A pale blue cotton dress with short sleeves and a white collar gave her a rather little girl look, she realised, but she was not inclined to change it again, and she was very hungry. Mrs. Leith had murmured something about a meal when she was ready, and whatever she was offered would be welcome.

As she left her room, she hoped she could find her way down to the dining-room. Mrs. Leith had indicated its location as she showed her to her room, but she was not certain if she could remember which one of the doors it was. The stairs were wide and airy, with gilded iron balustrades and shallow treads, and as Kate made her way down she was drawn to a portrait about half way down.

It was executed in oils and there was something familiar about the features of the subject that puzzled her—a grey-haired man with a broad high forehead and grey eyes, a hint of arrogance in the angle of the head had him looking down a prominent nose at the viewer, and Kate recognised him for who he was suddenly.

Leaning back against the balustrade she cocked her head to one side and considered the similarities between her own grandfather and what could only be his older brother, Charles. It was an excellent painting and showed the old man as he must have been about twenty years ago, about sixty years old and a strong arrogant character, used to having his own way, yet strangely at home against the background of delicate blossoms and bright blue sky.

She must have stood there admiring and studying for several minutes and she was aware of someone else just before she turned and looked down into the hall, drawn by another gaze. A man stood in the hall below looking up at her and appearing to be at a loss whether to speak to her or not.

He was medium height and somewhat stocky in build, with brown hair and light eyes, and he was dressed far more conventionally than the last man she had seen standing more or less where he was. A light blue shirt worn with a cream two-piece suit looked both cool and smart and he even wore a tie, which was something quite unexpected.

'Miss Wilmot?'

It was the second time she had answered that same query in the space of little more than an hour, but she did so this time less warily. Coming down the rest of the stairs, she smiled as she looked at the newcomer, and he proffered a hand. 'I'm Calvin Morton, Miss Wilmot, pleased to make your acquaintance!' He must have noticed her brief puzzled frown, for he hastily went on to explain, 'I'm—that is, I was Mr. Charles Wilmot's secretary.'

'Oh, I see!' Kate took the proffered hand and was pleasantly surprised by its firm grip. 'I'm glad to see you, Mr. Morton, there's quite a lot I'd like to ask you.'

She thought he looked vaguely uneasy, but she couldn't be sure. 'I don't know if I can be of much help,' he said. 'If it's to do with the estate, Miss Wilmot, Mr. Chang's the man to see about that.'

'I see.' Her disappointment must have been obvious, for Calvin Morton smiled encouragingly and just touched her arm with his finger-tips. 'I'm sorry about it, Miss Wilmot, but I really didn't know what the old—what Mr. Wilmot said in his will, which is what I presume interests you.'

'I'm concerned about sharing, or apparently being expected to share the house with a Mr. Fernandez,' Kate told him. 'I suppose you can't tell me anything about that, can you?'

He said nothing for a moment but guided her across the hall towards the door of the dining-room. 'I believe Mrs. Leith has a meal ready for you,' he told her, changing the subject without actually appearing to do so. 'You must be hungry.'

'I'm famished,' Kate agreed with a smile. 'I'm always far too excited to eat while I'm travelling and I've come nine thousand miles today!'

'Surely not on an empty stomach!' he exclaimed. 'But you *must* be famished!'

A meal was already laid on the long table in the dining-room and Kate noticed that she was evidently expected to eat alone, for there was only one place. 'Couldn't you stay and have something with me?' she asked, and Calvin Morton shook his head, although it was obvious that the invitation pleased him.

'No, thanks a lot,' he told her, 'I haven't long eaten. I really just came in to fetch the rest of my things, but I'm glad I've met you, Miss Wilmot.'

Kate looked at him curiously, realising for the first time that in a household like Charles Wilmot's the private secretary often lived in. Her own arrival must have inconvenienced him to quite an extent, but he had made no word of complaint, or even suggested he should stay on.

'You normally live here?' she asked, and he nodded.

'I have been while Mr. Wilmot was alive, of course,' he said. 'But naturally everything's different now.'

'I'm sorry.'

He looked at her for a moment, then smiled, a slow and quite attractive smile that did curious things to her pulses. 'You don't have to be sorry,' he told her. 'I could hardly stay on now that you'll be living here alone.'

Kate looked at him and frowned curiously. 'Alone?' she asked, and he nodded, obviously puzzled. 'But——' She tried to make sense of the information she had been given so far. 'I understood that the house belonged equally to Mr. Fernandez.'

'He owns part of it too,' Calvin Morton agreed. 'But he has the beach house below the cliff. The old man let him have it so that he could do those daubs of his, he doesn't live in the house itself.'

'Oh, I see!' Her relief was evident, and he smiled as he shook his head.

'Oh, I guess he'd move in if he thought he could get away with it,' he told her with surprising candour. 'But neither Mrs. Leith nor I would let him, so don't worry about it, he'll stay put in the beach house, though he might be around here during the daytime, I'm afraid.'

Kate smiled. 'I think I can cope with Mr. Fernandez,' she said with far more confidence than she felt. 'Although I suppose he does have the right to come and go as he pleases, since he had a half interest in the house.'

'Only a third, Miss Wilmot,' Calvin Morton corrected her quietly. 'I have an interest too.'

Kate's eyes were blank with disbelief as she gazed at him. Her dream house in the South Seas was rapidly becoming the property of all and sundry and she began to wonder if it had been worth all that long flight if she was to inherit no more than a third share in a house, no matter how beautiful and luxurious it might be.

'You didn't know that?' Calvin Morton asked

gently, and Kate shook her head.

It occurred to her suddenly that for a man who had claimed he knew nothing about the will he seemed very well informed about who owned the house at least. 'You—I thought you couldn't tell me anything about the will,' she said in a small and rather tired voice, and he shook his head, a smile on his rather good-looking face that took the edge off the words he spoke.

'I guess you have the know-how for prising information out of a man,' he told her, and somehow managed to make it sound like a compliment.

Kate liked that smile. It did even more attractive things to his nicely good-looking face and he was really much more restful than her other co-heir. 'I think I've a lot to learn about Uncle Charles,' she said. 'I only wish I'd known him.'

There was no mistaking the look in Calvin Morton's grey eyes as he looked at her, standing only a foot or so from her, neat and smart in his light suit. Then he took her hand without her really noticing he was doing it, and gazed deep into her eyes, so earnest and honest that she felt she trusted him instinctively. 'I guess I'm one up on him here,' he said softly. 'I *do* know you, and I'm very glad you came all those nine thousand miles, Miss Wilmot. From where I stand it was worth every mile!'

Kate smiled, a warm glow permeating her whole being as she allowed her hand to stay in his, regardless of Mrs. Leith bringing in dishes and plates, and the protesting grumbles of her empty stomach. Calvin Morton was not only a very attractive man

24

he could also be very helpful in the days to come.

'I'm Kate,' she said with an impulsiveness she could not resist, and he smiled again.

'My friends call me Cal,' he told her. 'And I hope we're going to be *good* friends, Kate!'

CHAPTER TWO

It was such a pity to waste even a single second by lying abed, Kate decided the next morning. She had slept well in the enormous and incredibly comfortable bed, and now she was ready to face her first full day in the islands. Her first day as part-owner of the beautiful house that stood poised above the sea, surrounded by the most colourful and exotic collection of blossoms she had ever seen.

Briefly, as she dressed, Kai Fernandez came into her thoughts and she frowned over the idea of his being a joint heir of Charles Wilmot's property. Calvin Morton was much more acceptable in the role and at the thought of him she smiled. Calvin Morton had been a pleasant surprise, and she hoped the fact that he had been conscious enough of propriety to move out of Hale Makai did not mean that she would be seeing less of him than she was bound to do of Kai Fernandez.

Impatiently dismissing the less comforting of her two co-inheritors, she took a last look at herself in the mirror. Kai Fernandez had assured her that she had no need of many clothes in her present surroundings, and for the moment she was prepared to accept that he was right, but she fully intended spending some of her newly acquired wealth on something a little more exotic than her present wardrobe.

For the moment, however, the simple little cotton shirtwaister she wore over a bikini was adequate for her needs and the green patterned cotton suited her admirably. She intended sampling the delights of that deserted golden beach below the cliff that she had glimpsed only briefly yesterday evening, and a swimsuit had been one essential item she had to bring along. It would be impossible to live so close to the dazzling Pacific and not go swimming almost every day.

Satisfied with the way she looked, she went downstairs to breakfast, and it was only as she crossed the hall to the dining-room that it occurred to her to wonder whether she would be breakfasting alone or not. Calvin Morton had mentioned that Kai Fernandez occupied a beach house; she had seen it briefly last night when she looked down on it, tucked away below the cliff, snug amid its own lush shrubbery, but she had no idea if he had the means of cooking for himself or if he came up to the house.

The question was resolved soon enough when she walked into the big sunny room, and she sighed inwardly. The wide glass screen doors were pushed wide open to the warm scented morning air, and a breakfast table was laid for two out on the balcony. A balcony that ran at ground level along the back of the house and overlooked the ocean where the land curved inwards to encompass a small bay.

The view it presented was breathtaking by any standards, but to Kate, accustomed to neat suburban houses and gardens, it was like stepping into another world and she feared she might wake at any minute and find it was all a dream. Clusters of blossoms of every colour invaded the balcony and against a background of blue sky and a sapphire sea the effect was stunning.

The mingled scents too were quite intoxicating and she breathed deeply at the heady concoction as she walked across the room. Much less attractive, however, was the prospect of breakfasting with Kai Fernandez and it was plain that it was now inevitable, for he already sat at the little white table, apparently enjoying his breakfast.

He half rose to his feet when she came into the room and Kate tried not to notice the dark gleam of appreciation that came into his eyes as they swept over her from head to foot in frank appraisal. He was rather more formally dressed than yesterday and the cream slacks he had on were clean and free of paint stains.

He wore both shoes and a shirt too, even though the former were no more than light sandals and the bright yellow shirt that exaggerated his tan was open almost as far as his waist. His presence there and his part in the scheme of things still puzzled her and she would have given much for the nerve to ask just how he came to be one of her uncle's heirs.

'Good morning!' He accompanied the greeting with a smile that revealed strong white teeth and somehow made him look slightly villainous.

'Good morning, Mr. Fernandez.' Kate sat down facing him and found the suggested intimicy of sharing breakfast with him over a small table curiously disturbing.

He glanced up and from his expression it was possible to surmise that he guessed how she was feeling. 'We mostly have an English breakfast,' he told her, taking up a last forkful of bacon and egg, 'but I'm sure Leith will oblige if you fancy something more exotic.'

'We?' Kate ignored the invitation to change the breakfast menu and frowned at him curiously.

He crooked his wide mouth into a lopsided smile as if he read suspicion into her question. 'I guess I still think of Charlie as alive and kicking,' he explained quietly. 'He was the kind of man you think of as going on for ever—it's hard to believe he's really gone.'

'You were fond of him!'

It was a statement, not a question, and Kate could not imagine what had possessed her to make it, but she believed it was true, and the expression on Kai Fernandez' dark features confirmed it. He had been fond of her uncle, though whether as a friend or simply as a patron she was as yet uncertain.

He poured out more thick black coffee and did not look at her until he raised the cup to his lips. 'I guess I was fond of him,' he agreed quietly.

Strange and disturbing thoughts were mulling around in her brain suddenly, thoughts she had no control over and which both discomfited and dismayed her. There was no possible reason for them, except that she had heard such tales about Charles Wilmot in his younger days, and there was a curious air of belonging about the man who sat facing her.

She could accept Calvin Morton's position in the household readily enough. He had been employed

29

as her great-uncle's personal and private secretary and a lot of wealthy men remembered their staff in their wills, but she was unable to make as much sense of where Kai Fernandez fitted in.

Why the old man should have taken this dark and rakish man into his household was a mystery, unless—— She hastily pulled herself up when she found herself remembering the strong painted features in the portrait of Charles Wilmot that hung on the staircase and comparing them with the face of the man who shared her breakfast table. It was a discomfiting possibility to face, but she might, sooner or later, be obliged to face it.

Mrs. Leith brought in more bacon and eggs and fresh toast for her, but her greeting was brief and formal and she did not even enquire whether Kate had passed a good night in her new home. It was plain, on the face of it, that for some reason best known to herself, Mrs. Leith did not care for either Kate or Kai Fernandez and she made little effort to conceal the fact.

It was curious, if she was indeed as disapproving as she appeared, that she had stayed on after her late employer died unless she too had reason to expect something from his estate. Kate had no idea how long she had been at Hale Makai, but her manner hinted at an almost proprietorial interest often found in long-serving staff.

Alone with Kai Fernandez again, Kate looked up and found him sitting with his hands clasped together one on top of the other, and his chin resting on them while he watched her steadily as she poured herself coffee. He smiled when she looked at him and inclined his head towards the cup of rich black brew in front of her.

'You might not like that,' he informed her. 'It's a bit too much for *malihini* tastes sometimes.'

Kate regarded it for a moment without committing herself. The coffee did indeed look much thicker and blacker than she was accustomed to, and she could already imagine the taste with sufficient clarity to make her shudder. 'I haven't tried it yet,' she told him. 'What's so special about it?' She was unwilling to appear so conservative that she refused to try anything new, especially when she was faced with that challenging, lopsided smile.

'It's called Kona,' he said. 'A special Hawaiian brew. Charlie liked it and we always drank it, except Cal Morton, of course, and he took his watered down with milk!'

It was obvious that he saw such practices as sacrilegious and Kate wondered if he had actually said as much to Calvin Morton. Unless she had misread the signs there was little love lost between the two men and it was not difficult to imagine two such opposites verbally sparring on occasion. He was probably waiting to be equally derisive about her own tastes.

She looked around the table. 'There doesn't appear to be any milk,' she told him, 'so it looks as if I haven't much choice.'

That crooked smile touched his mouth again and he raised a brow. 'I guess Leith's trying to see what stuff you're made of,' he remarked.

'I see!'

Kate thought Mrs. Leith wasn't the only one

waiting to see what she was made of, and she was prepared to swallow almost anything to defy the gleaming hint of challenge in those watching dark eyes. She stirred plenty of sugar into the coffee and found it quite to her liking; it wasn't bitter and she did not feel in the least like shuddering as she drank it.

'Good?' he asked, and Kate nodded.

'Quite pleasant,' she agreed, and held his eyes for a moment. 'Maybe I'm not quite like some of the—the *malihinis*,' she said. 'Whatever it means.'

He was regarding her steadily and she hastily looked away again. 'It means stranger or newcomer,' he said. 'Which is what you are at the moment, Miss Wilmot.'

Kate did not, as she had with Calvin Morton, invite him to use her christian name, and she was a little surprised that a man like Kai Fernandez did not take the onus upon himself. Something in his tone when he made the observation gave her the impression that he was trying to impress her with the fact that she was a foreigner, a *malihini* as he called it, and she instinctively resented it.

She made no secret of her study of him, and swept her gaze over the bold, dark features with an unmistakable glint in her own green eyes. 'It's obvious that you aren't a *malihini*, Mr. Fernandez,' she said in a cool voice, and felt the colour flush into her cheeks when he laughed.

He still sat with his hands clasped under his chin, his dark eyes watching her with a gleam in their depths that was more discomfiting than she cared to admit. 'I'm what we call *kamaaina*, Miss

Wilmot,' he said. 'I was born here.'

'Yes, of course,' Kate concurred. 'I realised that.'

She wished she knew what it was that was causing that bright gleam of amusement, but she hadn't the nerve to challenge him with it. 'Do you know Portmeirion?' he asked suddenly, and Kate blinked, bewildered for a moment by the unexpectedness of the question.

'Well—yes,' she said, frowning. 'It's in Wales.'

He nodded, still watching her and speculating on her reaction. 'My mother came from there,' he told her, and her obvious surprise drew another smile from him. 'Surprised?' he suggested softly, and Kate nodded, not sure whether to believe it or not, although heaven knew why he should lie about it.

'I—I am rather,' she confessed. 'I thought you were——' She hesitated to say 'native' in its less flattering context, and her hesitation seemed to give him further cause for amusement.

'This is the one place in the world, honey,' he informed her softly, 'where it's impossible to insult a man by referring to his race or colour. No one in these islands ever asks questions about such things because it simply isn't important. Only *malihinis* notice anything untoward about the thousand and one mixtures we come in, to us it doesn't matter.'

'Oh no, of course it doesn't,' Kate agreed hastily. 'I was just surprised because of your name, that's all.'

'Kai?' He pronounced it with both the 'a' and the 'i' as he had when he introduced himself. 'In fact my mother named me,' he told her. 'It's Welsh and she calls it Kiy, but coincidentally the Hawaiian word for sea or salt water is spelled in exactly the same way and——' he shrugged carelessly, 'to everyone but her I'm Kai.'

Kate found the explanation interesting enough to let down the barriers of her resentment while she listened to him and she wondered how much more forthcoming he would be—about his father for instance. 'I've never heard it before,' she told him, 'and I certainly didn't expect it to be Welsh!'

The dark eyes glowed as he regarded her for a moment and she felt suddenly and inexplicably nervous as she bore his scrutiny. 'Not that I see my mama very often, she doesn't approve of me any more than you do,' he said after a moment or two, and held up a hand before she could object to the supposition. 'Cal Morton will give you the low-down on me,' he went on with a suggestion of laughter in his voice, 'if he hasn't already! I'm a bad lot, Katie Wilmot, you ask Cal or Mrs. Leith, they'll tell you!'

For a second Kate said nothing, then she shook her head, giving her attention again to her meal. It struck her that unless she had misjudged him badly, Kai Fernandez would relish an unsavoury reputation rather than seek to deny it, but she still remembered the taxi driver on the way there coupling his name with that of her great-uncle, and she was not prepared to consider Charles Wilmot as anything other than the straightforward business man he had become in later life, no matter what he had been in his younger days.

'You were a—friend of my uncle's,' she said, 'and

I can't believe he'd have taken an interest, or taken you into his home if you'd been the—the bad lot you'd have me believe, Mr. Fernandez!'

'No?' He made the enquiry softly and his eyes glittered a challenge, as if her faith amused him. 'Don't go seeing Charlie Wilmot as a saint,' he said. 'If you think that you'll be doing him less than justice. He liked people and he loved life and he got the most he could out of both in his time, so don't give him a halo, honey, now he's gone—nor his friends!'

'I don't care about his friends, but he was my grandfather's brother,' Kate reminded him, as if she was honour bound to defend the old man who, for some curious and inexplicable reason, had decided at the end of his days to make the youngest member of his disapproving family one of his heirs.

'But I *knew* him!' Kai Fernandez declared quietly. 'You never even saw him!'

'I know that, but I simply won't believe he was as bad as you make him sound!' Kate insisted, and he shook his head firmly.

'Not bad,' he denied. 'Never! But he did a lot of things that conventional, stuffed shirt family of his wouldn't have approved, and he had the island gift of accepting a man as he is—that's why we got along.'

Kate studied the slice of toast she was buttering and did not look up. 'He presumably got on with Calvin—Mr. Morton too,' she suggested. 'And you and he haven't much in common that I can see.'

'Sure he got along with him,' Kai Fernandez agreed willingly. 'Like I said, he accepted a man for what he was, and Cal Morton's damned good at his job!'

The praise was unexpected and, Kate felt, sincere and it surprised her. She had expected him to be sarcastic about Calvin Morton, for it was obvious that the two of them would have nothing in common, and the man she had imagined Kai Fernandez to be would have despised anyone as conventionally formal as his co-inheritor. Instead he was unhesitant in his praise and obviously meant it. He was, she was bound to admit, far too much of an enigma for her to solve at the moment.

She ate her toast and drank the rest of her coffee, hoping that he would soon decide to leave her, for he had long since finished his own meal, but he seemed in no hurry to leave and simply sat watching her while she finished her own breakfast. 'Do you have any plans?' he asked as she put down her empty coffee cup, and Kate shook her head.

She would hate to appear rude when she refused his offer to be her guide, but she was almost certain that was what he had in mind and she would much rather be escorted by Calvin Morton. 'I shan't be going far from the house,' she told him. 'Mr. Chang, Uncle Charles' lawyer, is coming to see me today.'

'He's coming to see more than just you, honey,' he told her with a hint of a smile. 'You seem to forget, you aren't the only one with an interest in old Charlie's will.'

'No, no, of course not!' She got up from the table and stood for a moment looking down at him, wondering what else there was beside Welsh blood that gave him that strong, bold look. 'If you'll excuse me, Mr. Fernandez, I have things to do.'

'Oh, sure!' He leaned back in his chair and his dark eyes challenged her from between those effeminately long lashes. 'I get the message, honey!'

Kate, sensitive to the fact that she was being suspected of snobbery at the very least, took a deep breath and determinedly met his eyes. 'I wish you wouldn't call me honey, Mr. Fernandez,' she said quietly. 'I don't like it at all.'

'Oh, you don't?' His eyes glittered and he got to his feet suddenly and stood facing her across the sparse width of the little table, looking at her down the length of that impressively noble nose. 'Do you have any preference as to what you're called?' he asked, so quietly that it was evident he was controlling himself firmly, and Kate flushed.

'There's nothing wrong with Miss Wilmot, is there?' she asked in a betrayingly shaky voice.

For a second nothing happened, and then he laughed suddenly and unexpectedly, his head thrown back and the strong brown throat exposed. 'There's a whole lot wrong with Miss Wilmot,' he said, 'but nothing we can't do something about in time!'

He gave her no time to answer but with one last, glittering look turned and strode across the room without another word, and Kate followed his progress with vaguely uneasy eyes. It could scarcely have been termed a threat, but it made her shiver involuntarily just the same.

Mr. Robert Chang proved to be less awe-inspiring

than Kate had feared. He was a small, dark and only slightly Oriental-looking man with a bland expression that gave little away. He appeared to be on good terms with both Kai Fernandez and Calvin, and even Mrs. Leith put herself out to be pleasant to him.

The Englishness of Charles Wilmot's study was unexpected in a house that in every other respect was modern and keyed to a permanently sunny climate. The rest of the house might have light tropical furniture, but here the decor, the heavy three-piece suite and even the carpet had the look and feel of an English country house, and Kate found it oddly touching. It was as if he had tried to recreate a small corner of his native land in a world that was completely different.

It was no real surprise to find Mrs. Leith among those assembled for the reading of the will, but Kate thought she seemed unnaturally anxious as she sat beside Calvin on the old-fashioned velvet settee beside the window. Of the three principal heirs it was obvious that Calvin Morton was Mrs. Leith's favourite and Kate noticed how often she glanced at him while they waited for Mr. Chang to begin.

Thinking to appear more formal for such a solemn occasion Kate had put on a dark blue dress with long sleeves, and she sat in one of the huge wing armchairs with her hands in her lap, trying not to look too often at her companions. Even Kai Fernandez had put on a suit, though not a tie, and in some ways the more formal attire made him look more exotic than before.

His features were composed into a solemnity that Kate had not seen there before and he sat in the chair opposite her, leaning forward with his hands clasped loosely and easily together, his elbows resting on his knees. A white shirt gave him added darkness, especially in the shadows of the cool, shady room, and Kate could not help feeling that he looked completely alien in such English surroundings.

Calvin Morton, on the other hand, had the smooth, formal look of his kind all the world over. A neat light grey suit with a blue shirt and tie and smart, highly polished shoes. It was difficult to guess what was going on in his mind because his eyes were completely hidden by the light from the window falling on the rimless spectacles he wore. Something she had not noticed yesterday.

'Ladies and gentlemen?' Mr. Chang had their immediate attention, and once again Kate noticed a swift anxious glance at Calvin from the corners of Mrs. Leith's eyes. Her obvious anxiety was puzzling and Kate wondered about it briefly before she gave her attention to what was being said.

The preliminaries were meticulously gone through, word for word, and Kate curled her hands tightly into her palms as the moment approached. '*To Kate Elizabeth Wilmot, the granddaughter of my beloved Lizzie, I leave a third share in the property known as Hale Makai and a third share in the beach house, also the sum of four hundred thousand dollars, providing that she remains in Hawaii for a period of not less than one year after this will is read.*'

So there it was! A fortune, even translating the money into pounds sterling, and the only condition that she stay in the islands for a year. It was almost too much to believe and Kate was momentarily stunned by it so that she almost missed the rest of the reading.

There was, she thought vaguely, a swift intake of breath from Mrs. Leith, and Calvin was looking at her from across the room with a steady, strangely unbelieving look in his eyes. Kai Fernandez, she heard through a kind of haze, was to receive, beside his share in the two houses, five thousand dollars, and Calvin Morton a similar share in the property and ten thousand dollars.

It was when the last was announced that Kate became aware of the housekeeper's malevolent stare and blinked in surprise. Her own not inconsiderable share seemed not to matter at all to her, but she was taking up cudgels on Calvin Morton's behalf with a vehemence that was almost unbelievable.

'Ten thousand dollars!' she said harshly, looking at Robert Chang with equal malevolence. 'Ten thousand dollars while that—that woman from England gets a fortune! Why did you let him do it?' she demanded of Mr. Chang. 'You must have known what he meant to do—why didn't you stop him?'

'Mrs. Leith, please!' Mr. Chang tried to soothe her, his bland smooth features attempting a smile. 'It's very generous sum.'

'It's scandalous!' Mrs. Leith declared, her voice hoarse with anger. 'You know it is, Robert Chang!

There should have been more for him!' Once again her narrowed, brightly angry eyes turned on Kate and she almost spat the words at her. 'Just because he remembered a woman he couldn't have!' she rasped. 'Your grandmother!'

No longer able to dwell in her rosy dream, Kate found it difficult to believe that she was actually hearing the words, but there was nothing unreal about the flushed and angry face of the housekeeper, and it was equally certain that she objected violently to Kate's share in the estate.

What was most puzzling of all was why Mrs. Leith should put Calvin Morton's case with such passion when Calvin himself merely sat there beside her with a still and oddly distant look on his face. She could see now why she had not noticed the spectacles yesterday when they met, for he was taking them off again now and putting them carefully away in a leather case he took from his top pocket.

The action complete, he looked straight across at Kate and the expression on his good-looking face puzzled her further. His light grey eyes regarded her steadily and there was a curiously speculative look in them for a moment, then he smiled, a small, dry smile that barely touched his mouth and never reached his eyes at all.

'I'm quite satisfied with what I have,' he said quietly, apparently addressing himself to Mrs. Leith, although he was looking at Kate. 'Please don't fuss!'

'But——'

'No!' The command was made with such surprising vehemence that even Mrs. Leith winced away from it and subsided, although it was obvious that she was far from satisfied. 'I'm sorry, Mr. Chang,' Calvin said quietly. 'Please go on—there are one or two more bequests, aren't there?'

'There is the sum of five hundred dollars to go to a Frederick Leong,' Mr. Chang said. 'He is a taxi driver, I believe, and rendered Mr. Wilmot some service over the years.'

'He's a great little character,' Kai Fernandez said, and looked across at Kate. 'He brought you out here yesterday,' he reminded her. 'This little windfall will make his day!'

'It's a pity he wasn't as conscious of more important obligations!' Mrs. Leith interrupted harshly, and Kai gave her a slow, rueful smile.

'No one ever put one over on the old man!' he told her, and Kate registered with amazement the flush of hot colour in the housekeeper's thin cheeks as she glared at him malevolently.

It was plain that Mrs. Leith followed his rather oblique meaning, even if it completely bamboozled Kate, and Kate wondered if there had ever been a more eventful reading of a will. Her own world had changed completely in the space of a few seconds—as long as it took for Mr. Chang to read out the sum of four hundred thousand dollars.

Kate looked at Calvin Morton's pleasantly good-looking face through the thickness of her lashes and sought for the right words. After they left Charles Wilmot's curiously English study Calvin had lost no time in being at her side and she had no objection to the idea at all, except that she half feared some kind of a scene once they were alone.

It had been clear that the size of his inheritance had stunned him as much as it had Mrs. Leith, but he had refused to let the housekeeper make a public scene. Once they were alone he might be less reticent and Kate had no wish to quarrel with him.

'I—I feel as if I ought to say—well, something,' she told him as they walked down the wooden steps leading down to the beach. 'I mean about the will; Mrs. Leith seemed to think——'

'Mrs. Leith spoke out of turn,' he assured her with a hint of a smile. 'You don't have to worry your head about a thing, Kate, not a thing!'

It was a relief to find him ready to let the matter drop, but the housekeeper's astonishing outburst still needed some explanation. 'I don't understand her at all,' she confessed. 'She seemed to think that I'd deprived you of something, and I'd hate to come in, a stranger, and take what should rightfully be yours or anyone else's.'

His grey eyes, she could see on closer acquaintance, were probably quite weak and he should possibly have worn those spectacles all the time, but they were very nice, friendly and attractive eyes and she could understand his reluctance to hide them. He was smiling again too and it was a very attractive smile, as she had noticed yesterday, that made him look a lot younger than he did in his more serious moments.

'The old man was free to leave his property to whom he liked,' he told her, 'and you're his family, so who better? Now please——' He took her hand

43

and gently squeezed her fingers. 'Don't say another word about that darned money, O.K.?'

'O.K.!' Kate laughed, responding readily enough to both the gentle pressure on her fingers and the look in those nice grey eyes.

The setting was idyllic and she could think of nothing more inappropriate than quarrelling with a good-looking man in such surroundings. The sea was like crumpled blue silk, and in the distance a white boat sped across its surface leaving a wide, foam-edged vee in its wake.

Below them as they walked down the steps the little beach-house where Kai Fernandez lived snuggled into its lush and colourful garden at the foot of the cliff, leading straight out on to the broad golden sandy beach. Great billowing rollers swept in one after the other, huge and impressive, and further along the beach someone rode the surf, a small, delicately balanced figure with spread arms, a speck on the vastness of the ocean.

A ragged line of palms straggled across the beach from a lower level of vegetation and formed the traditional South Seas island picture, and Kate sighed, a deep, heartfelt sigh of sheer contentment, glancing up at her companion with a smile. 'It's going to be no hardship staying on here for a year,' she said. 'I shall probably *never* want to leave!'

Again those firm cool fingers squeezed hers and she realised for the first time that she was walking hand in hand with him and had been all the time. It seemed such a natural thing to do somehow. 'I hope you never will,' he said quietly. 'I sincerely hope you never will, Kate!'

CHAPTER THREE

MRS. LEITH was waiting for her in the hall one morning when Kate came down to breakfast, and Kate found her lying in wait for her rather ominous, although there was really no reason to suppose it was so. Usually her first glimpse of the housekeeper was when she brought in her breakfast, so that it was a pretty obvious conclusion that something was amiss, and Kate immediately thought of Kai Fernandez.

She had been avoiding him as far as possible the past few days, but there was no knowing what he might have done to arouse the ire of Mrs. Leith, anything was possible and now it seemed she was to hear about it. It was all so much supposition, of course, but the narrow grey eyes seemed to regard her with a certain malevolent satisfaction as she came downstairs and Kate's heart rapped anxiously at her ribs in anticipation.

A rather hesitant smile brought no more than a cold hard look in response and the thin figure was drawn up in stern discouragement. 'I'm giving notice,' Mrs. Leith told her without preliminary, and Kate stared at her blankly for a moment.

'You're——'

'Giving notice,' Mrs. Leith confirmed adamantly, as if she expected Kate to try and talk her out of it and was firmly resolved to be unmoved.

At the moment Kate could only think that Kai

Fernández was something to do with it and before she set about trying to persuade the housekeeper to stay she wanted to know what her reason was for leaving. 'If Mr. Fernandez has said or done something——' she began.

'Mr. Fernandez has nothing to do with it,' Mrs. Leith interrupted. 'I'm just quitting the job, that's all.'

'Oh, I see.'

There seemed little else she could say. The sudden decision was unexpected, and yet it shouldn't have been, for only five days ago Mrs. Leith had inherited ten thousand dollars under her late employer's will and such a sum entitled her to a long holiday at least. To Kate, however, it meant looking for a new housekeeper and she had to confess to complete ignorance in the matter of hiring and firing domestic staff.

'I'm sorry,' was all she could think of to say, and Mrs. Leith's mouth twisted in derision.

'You can't claim to be surprised,' she said. 'Not after that will!'

'Oh no, of course not!' Kate agreed, still not quite sure whether she had the right reason. 'You have some money now, Mrs. Leith, you should enjoy it, I don't blame you in the least. But if you could——'

'I'll stay the month,' Mrs. Leith interrupted again, her narrow eyes watching Kate closely. 'But you'd better start looking for somebody else.'

'Yes, of course—thank you.'

A bold front was best with someone like Mrs. Leith, Kate felt, but inwardly she dreaded the chore of replacing her. She was quite capable of doing her own housekeeping in other circumstances, but circumstances were hardly normal here. For one thing she knew nothing about dollars and cents, or about American/Hawaiian style shopping, and for another there was the problem of Kai Fernandez to consider. She couldn't face trying to keep house to his satisfaction, and presumably he would expect to go on having his meals at the house.

Someone would have to help, and it was while she was crossing the hall to the dining-room that she found what she thought should be the obvious solution. Calvin Morton was also a part-owner of Hale Makai and he would, she felt, be only too pleased to help her find another housekeeper. Seeing her problem almost solved she smiled as she walked into the long sunny dining-room, then almost immediately frowned when she saw Kai Fernandez in possession of the balcony table. One person she wished she could dispense with was her breakfast companion, but there seemed little prospect of that at the moment.

He got up from his seat when she came in and greeted her with the curious gesture that was half wave, half salute, before seating himself again, a small crooked smile on his face that made her wonder if he had overheard her exchange with Mrs. Leith. 'Good morning,' he said, setting the coffee down within her reach, and Kate inclined her head in acknowledgement.

The rakish dark eyes noticed every curve revealed by a brief cotton dress, she realised, and they glowed darkly at her obvious discomfiture. She sat down facing him and poured herself some coffee. 'Mrs. Leith's just given me notice,' she told him, hoping to surprise him as she had been surprised, but instead he smiled and shook his head.

'You're second in line, honey,' he told her. 'She saw me first!'

'Oh, I see!' Feeling rather deflated, she sipped her coffee, not really caring if Mrs. Leith had forgotten to cook her breakfast this morning, for she had not much appetite.

'I guess she means it to be official if she's given us both warning,' Kai said after a while. 'Seven years is quite a time, but it was only to be expected now.'

Sensing something in his voice, Kate looked at him curiously. 'Seven years *is* quite a long time,' she observed. 'She'll probably find it quite a wrench after all that time.'

'I guess,' Kai agreed quietly, and again something in his manner puzzled Kate. 'But she was bound to quit once the old man was gone.'

He sat with his elbows on the table, holding his coffee in both hands, and in that position he was necessarily brought closer to her with so little space available. Calvin Morton had nice, friendly grey eyes and she could meet them easily enough when she wanted to, but Kai Fernandez' were deep and unfathomable and she was never sure just what was going on behind them, so that she avoided looking at him whenever possible. They teased her, but they also frankly approved of her as a woman and she always felt there was so much more to the man than appeared on the surface.

48

'Do you think she's told Cal too?' she asked, giving a brief wary glance in the direction of the kitchen in case the subject of their discussion appeared unexpectedly, and Kai laughed.

He sipped his coffee for several seconds without answering, then shook his head. 'You really don't know, do you?' he asked, and Kate stared at him for a moment uncertainly.

She remembered how anxious and how angry Mrs. Leith had been on Calvin's behalf, and she thought she had an inkling of the reason now that she saw the look in those dark eyes opposite. 'I— that is, I wondered if they were connected in some way,' she ventured, aware that she could be about to make a complete fool of herself if she was wrong. 'I thought perhaps there was some connection between Cal and Mrs. Leith,' she explained, and again Kai was smiling, a slow, speculative smile that glittered at her across the top of his coffee cup.

'As close as can be,' he said softly. 'She's his mother.'

'His——' She turned in time and saw Mrs. Leith coming in with her breakfast. Too stunned to know what else to do, she stared down at her breakfast when it was put in front of her for several seconds before she recovered sufficiently to look across at Kai again, only half believing.

'Didn't you guess that from the scene the other day when the will was read?' he asked before she could question him, and she shook her head vaguely.

'I—I guessed there was probably something,' she admitted, 'but I didn't realise—I mean, I'd no idea

49

she was his mother!'

It was still very hard to grasp, and she sat for several seconds trying to see something in Cal that bound him as closely as that with the housekeeper. Mrs. Leith's fierce defensive attitude was in complete accordance with a mother-and-son relationship, if she thought back, but she had seen little of affection in Calvin's attitude towards the woman Kai claimed was his mother.

'Maybe the name fooled you,' Kai suggested quietly.

'The name?'

He nodded. 'Ten years ago Mama Morton married a Mr. Leith, that's how come they're different. He died only three years later and that's when Cal came over from the mainland to be with her.'

'Oh, I see.'

There was something somewhere in the apparently quite simple situation that made her uneasy, but for the moment she was unable to decide what it was. She would like to have known more about Calvin, but it was unthinkable to ask Kai about him, especially when Calvin had made no secret of the fact that he disliked him intensely.

'Hasn't he told you anything about himself?' Kai asked, and Kate shook her head.

'Not that I've asked,' she said, and looked at him for a moment curiously. 'You appear to know a great deal about what goes on.'

Kai laughed, his dark eyes challenging her to put her curiosity into words. 'I'm *kamaaina*,' he reminded her. 'I hear all the island gossip!'

'So it seems!' If he knew so much about island

gossip, it suddenly occurred to Kate, he probably knew a great deal more about her uncle than he had said so far, and she studied him for several seconds through her lashes, debating on the wisdom of asking questions about that particular subject. 'You— you knew my uncle pretty well, didn't you?' she asked after a while, and Kai gave her a brief narrow-eyed look before he answered.

'Better than most, I guess,' he agreed quietly, but volunteered nothing more, so that Kate was left with the option of either asking questions or leaving it there.

'I was wondering——' she began, and hesitated, licking her lips anxiously while Kai watched her, slowly sipping his coffee. 'I wondered if—why Mrs. Leith expected Uncle Charles to leave Cal so much more than he did in his will.'

Kai finished his coffee and helped himself to more, and he took so long answering that Kate began to think he had no intention of answering her at all. 'I guess you'd better ask either Cal or Mrs. Leith that one, honey,' he said quietly at last. 'I might listen to gossip, but I try not to pass it on.'

'Oh, but I didn't——' She stared at him, appalled that he saw her natural curiosity as a desire to gossip, and her appetite was gone suddenly. She pushed away her half-empty plate and hastily dabbed her mouth while she looked at him with wide, reproachful eyes as she got to her feet. 'I wasn't asking you to pass on gossip,' she told him in a shaky voice as she stood by the little table looking down at him. 'You have no right to suggest I was prying —I wasn't!'

51

'I didn't suggest you were prying,' Kai argued quietly. 'You don't have to get so upset, for heaven's sake. Sit down and finish your breakfast.'

'I don't want any more!' She wanted to simply walk away, but her legs felt strangely weak and he was still watching her with those dark, disturbing eyes.

'You're mad at me,' he observed quietly, and half smiled as if the idea amused him.

Kate's fingers curled tightly into her palms and she felt her pulses thudding heavily as she faced him. 'I'm not—mad at anybody,' she denied. 'I simply don't want any more breakfast and I happen to be going out, so if you'll excuse me, I haven't much time!'

'You're seeing Cal?'

Kate spun round again and glared at him. The question was so softly asked that she had only just heard it, but he had no right to question her about whether she was seeing Calvin or not and she resented it. Her green eyes sparkled with resentment and she stuck her chin in the air as she faced him.

'Yes, I'm meeting Cal,' she agreed. 'Though I don't quite see what it has to do with you—unless of course you want to pass on *that* bit of island gossip too!'

'Tcch, tcch!' He shook his head at her, the glitter in his eyes belying the solemn expression he wore. 'That was real mean, honey, and you shouldn't be so ready to cut me down to size, you might be glad to have me around one day.'

Kate stuck out her chin, her soft mouth tightened into a firm straight line. 'It's unlikely!' she retorted, and walked out of the room.

The sand was warm and only slightly gritty between her toes and Kate felt she hadn't a care in the world at the moment. The warm sun and the sea, the palms and the houses high up on the blossom-shrouded cliffs were a dream world and she could ask for no one better to share it with than Calvin.

He walked beside her, his fingers just touching her, not quite holding hands but making her aware of his proximity by that delicate, almost erotic touch as they walked along the quiet beach. There was no one about, although she caught sight of Kai back near the beach house as they set out, hastily averting her eyes when she guessed he was watching them and lifting her chin in defiance of his opinion.

Beside them the sea surged in in those huge combers, the surf running in over the sand in a pattern of lace-edged foam, before being drawn back into its own element. Somewhere further along the inevitable solitary figure rode in on the surf, arms spread, a speck of brown-skinned humanity defying the glittering combers, balanced on a single tiny board.

Kate followed its progress with envious eyes as the surfer came to rest on the beach, having completed another successful run, and she laughed and shook her head. 'Whoever that man is he seems to spend all his time surfing,' she remarked. 'He must be well nigh perfect by now.'

Calvin's shoulders under a bright blue shirt shrugged almost contemptuously as he followed her gaze. 'Probably somebody with nothing better to do,' he said. 'It's a popular way of showing off.'

'Don't you approve?' she asked, and smiled up at him as she asked. 'I would have thought you would have tried it yourself.'

'No, thanks!' Calvin retorted shortly. 'I leave the showing off to people like Fernandez!'

In her mind's eye Kate could see Kai Fernandez emulating the graceful and daring antics of the man on the surfboard, and she could see too that Calvin would regard such behaviour as showing off, although in all fairness Kai probably wouldn't. She wore a bathing suit under her dress and wondered if today was a good time to make the acquaintance of the bright blue Pacific for the first time.

Although she had worn her swimsuit before she had never yet ventured into the water, being deterred by the sight of those huge rollers, now, in the company of Calvin, she might at last be able to venture in. She looked up at him and smiled. 'I suppose you aren't prepared for a swim, are you?' she asked, and he looked down at her and smiled.

'As it happens, I am,' he told her. 'Are you?'

'Always!' She laughed and already had the top button of her dress undone. 'I can be ready in two seconds!'

'O.K.!'

In a little more than two seconds they were actually in the water and Kate thought she had never felt such warmth. There was no sudden chill, such as she was used to in English waters, but a soft, tingling warmth like a bath, and she laughed aloud as she went further in.

Calvin in a pair of blue swimming shorts looked almost as light-skinned as she did herself, and she wondered if he spent very much time outdoors, or if he despised the Hawaiian craze for the outdoors as much as he seemed to dislike so much else to do with the islands. He looked more youthful without his formal clothes too, and she guessed he was very little more than her own twenty-two years, perhaps no more than three or four years.

Splashing about happily, she lost sight of him for several seconds, then saw him going further out and decided to follow him, calling as she went for him to wait for her. It was surprising how quickly it got deeper and she had lost sight of him again when she stood up and looked around.

'Cal!' she called out, but the sound of the water was enough to dull and flatten her voice into no more than a faint flutter of sound that died almost at once. 'Cal!'

Perhaps he couldn't hear her, but certainly he didn't answer, and she went on, determined not to be left behind if he was seeking to challenge her by going further out. She was not a very strong swimmer, but she was good enough to keep up with any average swimmer and she did not mean to be left behind.

The sand was soft under her bare feet and she was still in no further than her waist so that she was not in the least nervous and still searched the water for Calvin somewhere nearby. It was as if some gigantic monster had suddenly appeared when she turned her head and saw the comber bearing down on her, and she screamed as much in surprise as alarm.

The huge curl of water came with breathtaking speed and she had no chance to avoid it or to get out of its path before it engulfed her, arms and legs flailing helplessly, tossing her up and over as if she was no more than a lifeless doll. She was rolled over and over, her lungs bursting as she fought helplessly against the drag of the surf when the water returned to gather itself for another assault.

A thousand and one things ran through her mind as she was dragged down, and the most vivid sensation was one of regret that she had had time to do so little with her life as yet. The Pacific paradise had proved that it could be not only beautiful but frightening too, and her last conscious thought was that all the people who would grieve most for her were more than nine thousand miles away.

For some time before she opened her eyes Kate was hazily conscious of a sequence of sounds, and of one sound in particular—a deep, heavy sound of breathing that was somehow connected with her own breath-rhythm. Her heart felt as if it was thudding away for dear life and as she began to remember and panic, another mouth was pressed over hers and the force of a deep, warm breath entered her lungs and shuddered through her whole being.

She stirred, turning her head from side to side and making a small, soft sound of protest, and something beside her moved, a voice not even a whisper, breathing words that sounded very much like a brief prayer of thanks to a merciful deity. Then she opened her eyes and found Kai Fernandez on his knees beside her, his dark features looking like chiselled bronze and gleaming wetly with sea water.

She looked at him for a long breathless moment, trying to understand the look of sheer relief in his eyes, then she took a long shuddering breath of her own volition, and turned her head away. 'Cal?' she asked in a hoarse whisper. 'Is he——'

'Alive and kicking,' Kai replied shortly, and got to his feet in one swift, easy movement, standing for a moment in the sand beside her.

He was fully dressed she saw when she turned her head again, or as fully dressed as he ever was, with nothing at all covering his golden brown upper half and only a pair of thin white cotton trousers clinging tightly to his long legs with the dampness that lent the rest of his body an oiled and gleaming look.

She found the scrutiny of those dark eyes too much to hold for very long and again turned away, looking up at the sky like a vast bale of blue silk shimmering with golden overtones. Everything, she thought hazily, was golden in these islands— the sand, the sky, even the people, most of all the people—people like Kai Fernandez who looked as smoothly golden as a pagan statue as he stood over her.

'Do you feel like moving now?'

She lay for a moment without answering, a strangely pleasant sense of lethargy making her inactive, lying back on the sand, her limbs relaxed and heavy. 'I suppose so,' she said after a second or two, and he reached down his hands for her.

She would have taken them willingly, but at the same moment Calvin appeared, bending down beside her, his good-looking face drawn and anxious and pale as death under the beading dampness of sea water. He knelt by her, his grey eyes searching her face, his hands taking hers and squeezing her fingers as if he could not quite believe she was alive.

'Oh, thank God!' he whispered, pressing her fingers to his mouth in an agony of relief. 'Thank God you're safe!'

'It's certainly no thanks to you!' Kai's voice broke into her half-formed answer, and Kate turned her head again swiftly, detecting something, some disturbing implication in his voice.

'You—you pulled me out,' she said, not for a moment doubting it, and he did not answer at once but looked across her at Calvin, who still held her fingers tightly in his and refused to meet the challenge.

'I'm used to the surf,' Kai told her. 'But anyone who's been in these islands more than five minutes should know how easy it is to get out of your depth until you're used to it.'

The accusation was unmistakable and she felt the fingers holding hers tighten, but Calvin knew when he was faced with a losing battle—he said nothing. 'I—I followed him in,' she said, her throat still sore and husky from the salt water. She used Calvin's clasping hands to pull herself to her feet and stood on alarmingly unsteady legs looking at her rescuer. 'You can't possibly blame Cal for what I did.'

The dark steady eyes held hers for longer than she found comfortable, then he laughed shortly, shaking his head and running one hand through his wet black hair. 'I don't blame anyone for what you did,' he told her. 'I only blame him for not warning you that you *could* get swept up by the combers if you didn't realise what you were doing.'

'*You* could have warned me too!'

Heaven knew what perverse streak of resentment made her make such a statement, especially to a man who had just pulled her out of the sea and saved her life, but her whole body was shivering with some inexplicable sense of panic when she thought of how he had revived her and she could not meet his eyes again, even in defiance.

He said nothing, and for several breath-stopping seconds they stood like statues on that stretch of golden sand. Then Kai turned and was moving away before she properly realised it and she remembered she had not even said a word of thanks to him for what he had done.

His long legs, the muscled calves outlined by the clinging wet cotton trousers, strode up the beach, his black head angled in such a way that it was easy to see he was angry. Kate watched him for a few seconds, standing beside Calvin, her hands clenched at her sides, then she impulsively ran after him, her legs still oddly weak and her feet dragged by the clinging sand.

'Kai!' He did not turn, but went on his way towards the house, half hidden by its exotic vegetation, his broad brown back firmly turned on her. 'Kai—wait!'

She had run after him almost half way up the beach before he finally turned and looked at her, and she faltered in the last few feet when she met the bright, glittering look in those dark eyes. His chest moved rapidly as if he was almost out of breath, but she realised after a moment that it was anger that made him so breathless, not haste, and she stopped, still a couple of feet away, her eyes uncertain.

He said nothing and she found it hard to find words to say what she had to say in the face of such obvious contempt. 'I——' She spread her hands in a gesture of helplessness and her eyes appealed to him for understanding. 'I haven't said a word of thanks,' she said huskily, conscious suddenly of her air of dishevelment. 'I should have thanked you, and I'm—I'm sorry I was so—ungrateful.'

'Are you?'

The soft-voiced question sent a warning shiver along her spine and she curled her hands tightly into fists as she stood there. Sand clung to almost every inch of her body, including the brief yellow bikini she wore, and her hair was damp and tossed into a rumpled mass that clung to her neck and her cheeks.

Putting both hands to her hair, she lifted it from her neck in a half conscious effort to make it appear less limp and lifeless, then she brushed the sand from her body with hands that trembled alarmingly. 'I—I am grateful, Kai,' she said throatily. 'Please believe me, I am.'

It was so hard not to remember that he had breathed life back into her only minutes ago, that

he had knelt beside her in the sand and forced her
lungs to start work again by giving her his own
life's breath. 'Show me!'

The words were unexpected and she blinked at
him uncomprehendingly for a second, then shook
her head. 'I don't know what——'

'Show me how grateful you are,' Kai interrupted, and his eyes flicked briefly in the direction
of Calvin standing further down the beach before
returning to fix themselves inmovably on her
mouth. His smile had a glittering wolfish look that
showed his strong white teeth and gleamed in his
eyes as he watched her.

Then he laughed suddenly and shook his head,
his eyes travelling the whole length of her, rakishly
appreciative but at the same time contemptuous of
her hesitation. 'Forget it!' he said shortly, and
turned on his heel. 'I don't take candy from
babies!'

'Kai!'

She was trembling as she called to him, angry
because he had challenged her, made her appear
like a naïve schoolgirl afraid of letting herself go. It
was obvious what he had expected of her and she
had behaved as if she did not follow his meaning,
was too inhibited to do as he expected.

He turned again, slowly, and looked at her with
those dark unfathomable eyes and she hesitated
only briefly, then went to him and raised herself on
tip-toe, her hands pressed to the smooth dampness
of his chest as she reached up for his mouth, her
own soft and hesitant.

Briefly he stood there, unmoving, while she

kissed him, then his hands moved suddenly and she was pulled hard against him, the golden warmth of his body pressed close until her own flesh quivered from the contact and she felt the muscular effort that sought to draw her even closer. His mouth was hard, warm and incredibly erotic so that she allowed it to go on for far longer than a mere gesture of thanks would have done.

He released her at last and she stood for a moment, breathing deeply and unevenly, as if she had run too far too fast. Then she looked up at him, her eyes wide, not quite believing she had been a party to such blatant seduction until she saw the glittering, half amused look in his eyes.

Angry as much with herself as with him, she pushed herself away from him and stood trembling, her legs too weak to run for several seconds before Calvin's angry voice from further down the beach brought her back to reality. She took one last look at that dark, pagan face and turned and ran, back down to the beach to Calvin's more comforting presence.

Two things she had learned about living in the islands today—one was never to get out of her depth in the surf, and the other never to give Kai Fernandez the opportunity to put her in debt to him.

CHAPTER FOUR

KAI suggested at breakfast one morning that she might like to see something of the history of Hawaii and Kate could hardly deny that she found the idea intriguing, although she had done her best to avoid being in his company for too long during the past few days.

None the worse for her near drowning, she still felt discomfitingly uneasy whenever she thought about his price for rescuing her, and Calvin had been so furious about that one kiss that it was evident he had similar ideas himself. He would probably have taken her to see the same museum that Kai proposed taking her to, but despite the fact that she usually felt more at ease with Calvin, she thought she might find it more interesting with Kai as her guide.

For all he claimed that his mother was Welsh, Kate still saw him as a complete islander, and she had so far heard no reference to his father. His accent was a kind of cultured American, although an occasional long 'a' betrayed his mother's British background, she thought, but she knew he conversed as easily in the mysterious and garbled speech of the islanders too.

She had been woken from sleep one night by the sound of a car on the drive and had been unable to resist a hasty look out of the window to confirm her suspicion that Kai was returning from a evening out. The car had proved to be a taxi, Freddie Leong's, she suspected, and the parting exchange between driver and passenger had taken place in completely incomprehensible pidgin English, and accompanied by gales of uninhibited laughter.

Pidgin was the common language of the less educated islanders, so she understood from Calvin, although the more élite would effect to copy it on occasion, but few people could have conversed in it with such ease, she felt, except a native islander, like Kai.

She looked at him now through the concealment of her lashes and for the thousandth time since her arrival wondered just who and what he was. She had not yet altogether ruled out the possibility of his being her great-uncle's son from some early liaison, but she was less sure of her suspicions now that she knew his mother was Welsh. There was something somewhere in his ancestry that gave him that dark, primitive look that was at once both disturbingly attractive and oddly disquieting.

She did not even stop to consider what Calvin's reaction would be to her spending a whole morning in Kai's company, for she was a free agent and owed allegiance to no one. Calvin's barely concealed jealousy was flattering, but she had no intention of letting it inhibit her actions nor influence her choice of company.

'How should I dress for this visit to a museum?' she asked, and Kai smiled.

She wore a simple pink print dress with no sleeves and a low scoop neckline, and Kai took stock of it with one of those bold, expressive looks

64

that she seemed never to get used to, no matter how often it happened. 'There's nothing wrong with what you're wearing now,' he told her. 'Haven't you learned yet, honey, that nobody dresses to kill here unless it's for one of those social drags that the upper crust indulge in from time to time?'

'Then I'll come as I am,' Kate decided, ignoring his comment of the social drawbacks, as he saw them.

He appeared more formally dressed than usual himself, so evidently even he had some standards to which he conformed on occasion, and she studied him again from the shadow of her lashes. The brown torso that was usually so blatantly exposed was covered by a gaudy silk shirt with short sleeves, but it was opened in front and he wore it loose over hip-hugging white drill trousers, the broad golden smoothness of his chest becoming visible whenever he leaned forward.

His thick black hair was tidily groomed for once, although it was already beginning to fall across his brow into its more customary careless style; and an expensive-looking gold wristwatch encircled one strong brown forearm, lending an unexpected touch of luxury. Something she had noticed before occurred to her again as she looked at him—that the more conventional clothes he wore the more they seemed to stress that dark, primitive air about him that was possibly his most disturbing feature.

'You seem to have dressed for the occasion,' Kate ventured, and he looked at her steadily for a moment over the rim of his coffee cup, his dark eyes glittering.

'I don't *always* look like a beachcomber,' he told her, and laughed, shaking his head slowly when she looked about to protest. 'I'd love to know exactly what you see me as, Kate,' he said, spreading one large hand palm upwards as he asked each question. 'Am I a beach-bum? A leech who saw old Charlie as an easy meal ticket? Maybe a wastrel from a good family or——?' His teeth gleamed whitely in the strong features and deep creases appeared at the corners of his wide mouth when he smiled. 'What am I, Kate? Do you really know?'

'I don't *want* to know!' Kate retorted, unexpectedly affected by that smile and swiftly on the defensive. 'I'm not sufficiently interested to even care who or what you are!'

It was a lie, she knew it, and from his expression he might have known it too, for he was shaking his head again and the smile still stayed in place, teasing her, like the bright glitter in his eyes. '*Nani* but *paakiki*,' he murmured softly. 'You sure are an unfriendly little devil, Katie Wilmot, don't you ever let up?'

'Not while you keep using Hawaiian words I don't understand!' Kate told him shortly. 'What was that you called me?'

'Beautiful but—pigheaded,' he translated obligingly. 'And that's just exactly what you are!' His eyes gleamed and he cocked a black brow at her as he spoke. 'I sometimes think the old Hawaiians had the right idea about women,' he added, and Kate frowned curiously.

It was such obvious bait to make her ask questions, and yet her curiosity made her willing enough to fall for it. 'What ideas were those?' she asked, and Kai laughed, leaning forward to rest his elbows on the table in front of him.

As always happened, his coming so close disturbed her senses more than she cared to admit and without realising she was doing it she instinctively sat more upright on her own chair and tried not to notice the broad golden chest exposed by the open shirt or the strong hands that had only to reach out and touch her.

'I'm talking about the original Hawaiians,' he told her, 'the Polynesians. Did you know that the ancient Hawaiian laws forbade women to even sit at the same table as the men, and all the choicest foods were *kapu* to them?'

Kate, certain she was being drawn into something she would later regret, took a moment to ponder while she finished buttering her toast and poured more coffee. 'That sounds pretty typical,' she remarked, much more interested in the possibility of him being at least part Polynesian himself. 'Do you have Polynesian blood?' she asked, and Kai shook his head, his smile seeming to mock her curiosity.

'Unfortunately no,' he admitted. 'But I'm *kamaaina*, honey, make no mistake about that! I belong here!'

'And I don't!' It was amazing how much she resented his reminding her and her green eyes shone with it as she looked at him. 'You never tire of reminding me I'm a mere *malihini*, do you, Kai?' she asked, but he refused to be drawn. 'Well, my uncle

67

was just as much a stranger to begin with as I am,' she went on, 'but you accepted him willingly enough, so why keep reminding me? Or do you support the old Hawaiian laws? One law for the men and another for the women?'

'Do I keep reminding you?' Kai asked quietly, and apparently quite seriously. 'I didn't realise I did!'

'In various ways.' She shrugged, unable to pinpoint any specific occasion apart from that first time when he had introduced her to the word *malihini*. 'I know I have a lot to learn about island ways,' she went on, determined to make her point, 'but I *will* learn, Kai, and I shall be here for at least another year, so you might just as well get used to me!'

For a moment he said nothing, but the dark eyes studied her carefully, slowly, taking in every feature from the nut-brown hair that curled about her shoulders to the small round chin that stuck out defiantly and the bright, uneasy green eyes that refused to quite meet his. 'Oh, I don't think that'll be too difficult,' he said at last, and before she realised his intention he leaned across the table and kissed her firmly, full on her mouth. Then he laughed softly and got to his feet. 'Now if you're coming with me,' he told her, 'be ready in about fifteen minutes, Katie. O.K.?'

The Hawaiian Hall in the huge Bishop Museum in Honolulu proved so fascinating that Kate would have liked to stay there all day regardless of how much else there was to see, and there were a great many other attractions. Kai proved to be an excellent guide, as she had expected, and it was obvious that the history of the islands was a consuming passion with him.

He told her so much more than Calvin could have done, and with such enthusiasm that it was bound to hold her interest. He pointed out the regalia of the old chiefs and told her about the fabulous feather cloaks, many hundreds of years old and painstakingly made from thousands and thousands of red and yellow feathers taken from birds that were now extinct. Only one feather was used from each bird, so that the capes and cloaks sometimes took years to make.

They were magnificent and quite unique and Kate had no difficulty imagining that Kai would have looked very much at home in the costume. The brief, brightly patterned *malo* or loincloth once worn by Hawaiian men and the feather-covered crested helmet, with the feather cloak of the chieftain hung about his broad shoulders— Polynesian or not, he had the necessary arrogance and carriage for the role.

Kate was easily drawn into the atmosphere in Kai's company and for a moment she took a step back in history, touched by something of the mystery and the magic of Hawaii. Much more so than if Calvin had been her guide, for Calvin had no rapport at all with the islands, nor wanted to.

'It's fascinating,' she whispered as they stood admiring one particularly splendid cloak, and Kai laughed softly.

'I thought you'd like old Hawaii,' he told her. 'It

appeals to that romantic imagination of yours, doesn't it, Kate?'

'Don't laugh at me!' It was too near the truth for her to take his teasing lightly, and she turned and looked at him reproachfully. But there was something else besides laughter in his eyes, something deep and unfathomable that made her turn away again hastily, her heart rapping hard at her ribs.

'I'm not laughing at you, honey,' he said softly, and the strong fingers on her bare arm tightened momentarily. 'Who am I to shatter your illusions?'

'That's a very good question,' Kate told him a little breathlessly. '*Who* are you, Kai?'

He said nothing for a second, then glanced at a male model wearing the traditional dress and smiled slowly. 'A little of several things,' he said quietly. 'Like most of the people who make up modern Hawaii.' He looked down at her for a moment, his eyes dark and unreadable, then he shook his head and the fingers on her arm urged her along to another exhibit. 'Just to show you it wasn't all hulas and moonlight,' he told her lightly, 'take a look at the bloodthirsty side of Hawaiian culture for a change!'

Kate only reluctantly broke the spell of a moment before, but her interest was still as keen and she obediently followed his suggestion to look at the darker side of what might at first sight appear to be Paradise. An incredibly ugly idol carved in wood had once been, so Kai informed her, the recipient of human sacrifice, and there was also a drum once used in a *heiau* or temple, ornamented with the grisly relics of human teeth.

It was an impressive but shivery display and quite involuntarily Kate found herself holding tightly to Kai's arm as they looked at it. 'Still think it's romantic?' he asked in a whisper close to her ear, and showed his own excellent teeth in a broad grin when Kate shook her head.

'No, of course it isn't *all* romance,' she said. 'It isn't reasonable to expect anything to be that, but it's very interesting and I'm glad I came.'

'You'd find it easier to give your imagination full rein with me alongside rather than Cal, of course,' he teased, and Kate pulled free of his hand, frowning.

'Maybe,' she agreed. 'Because he's *malihini*, like me!'

Stepping back hurriedly, she almost collided with someone coming up behind her and turned hastily to apologise. But before she could say a word the woman she had been about to apologise to reached out a hand and placed it on Kai's arm, smiling. She was plump, blonde and middle-aged, but the look she gave Kai was coquettish enough to appear coy and she obviously had no inhibitions about letting everyone hear her.

'Kai! Honey, we haven't seen you in ages— where *have* you been?'

Her voice shrilled through the surrounding crowd and Kate felt sure she would have embraced him if Kai had not taken discreet but definite steps to avoid her. The tightness of his smile showed how much he regretted the meeting, and in particular that shrill and penetrating voice. 'Mrs. Van Koren,' he said quietly. 'How are you?'

'If you lived in your own home, as you should, you wicked man, you'd know how we all are!' the woman told him with mock severity. 'Why do you hide yourself away like that?'

Kai's dark eyes held a glint of mockery as he looked at her and his wide mouth twitched into a suggestion of a smile. 'Because I like peace and quiet,' he said frankly, and for the first time the bright, curious blue eyes appeared to notice Kate.

A smile, more speculative than sweet, spread across the plump cheeks and Kate guessed that her being with Kai was about the last thing Mrs. Van Koren wanted to see. She was surely past the age when she considered herself attractive to a man like Kai, and yet there was a curious air of propriety about her when she spoke to him.

'How interesting!' she said with obvious meaning, and proffered a smooth white hand, weighed down with the most incredible collection of rings Kate had ever seen. 'I'm Clara Van Koren, my dear, and since this wicked man doesn't seem to be going to introduce us, we'd better introduce ourselves!'

Kate took the proffered hand and found its clasp surprisingly strong, but it was Kai who took the onus of introduction upon himself at last. 'This is Kate Wilmot,' he said briefly, and Kate saw Clara Van Koren's pencilled brows rise.

'Charlie Wilmot's——'

'Niece,' Kai interposed neatly, and his eyes sparkled as if he was enjoying the situation. 'His great-niece, to be exact, isn't that right, Kate?'

'That's right,' she agreed, and looked at Mrs. Van Koren curiously. 'Did you know my great-uncle, Mrs. Van Koren?'

'Oh, but of course, my dear!' A girlish giggle emerged from behind the hand she pressed to her mouth, and her eyes flicked briefly upwards in obvious insinuation. '*Every*one knew Charlie Wilmot!'

There was something in the way it was said, something about this blonde, simpering woman that Kate disliked intensely and she felt the colour that warmed her cheeks as she stuck out her chin. 'Unfortunately I didn't know him,' she said, 'but he was my grandfather's older brother and I can't think there can have been so much difference between them, Mrs. Van Koren!'

'Maybe not!' She shrugged plump shoulders and it was evident from Mrs. Van Koren's expression that she considered Kate was no longer a subject of interest and turned instead to Kai once more. 'Oh, that reminds me, honey,' she told him, 'I was speaking to Belle Kildair about you just yesterday, and she said to be sure and remind you, if I saw you, about two weeks Thursday!'

'Two weeks Thursday!' Kai struck his forehead dramatically and groaned. 'Of course—it's time for Belle's annual ball again, I'd forgotten!'

'You'll be there?' Mrs. Van Koren asked anxiously, and Kai shrugged. 'Oh but, Kai honey,' she protested, 'you must!'

'I guess I must!' He looked down at Kate and smiled. 'I'd hate to hurt Belle's feelings, she's a great gal, and I always do go to her annual get-together.'

'Then you'll be there?' Mrs. Van Koren insisted anxiously, and Kai nodded.

'I'll be there,' he agreed resignedly. 'I'll ring her.'

'Oh, I just *knew* you would!' The plump, heavily jewelled hands clasped together earnestly. 'You'd never let us down, I told Belle so—two weeks Thursday, now don't you forget!'

Kai glanced again at Kate and his dark eyes swept rapidly over her face as he smiled. 'I'll also be bringing myself a partner,' he said quietly, and Kate's heart gave a sudden crazy lurch.

'You'll——' Mrs. Van Koren's baby blue eyes narrowed sharply and she looked at Kate with unmistakable suspicion. 'Marjie will be coming,' she told Kai, as if it was bound to make him change his mind, but he merely inclined his head.

'Good,' he said. 'The more the merrier!'

'But, Kai honey——'

'O.K., I'll tell Belle myself,' Kai said, refusing to listen to arguments, and Kate was still trying to bring herself down to earth when Mrs. Van Koren's plump back disappeared into the crowd around the exhibits.

Unless she had failed to follow the conversation of the past few minutes correctly she had been invited to a ball of some kind, apparently whether she wanted to go or not, but that was fairly typical of Kai Fernandez. It would not even occur to him to ask if she wanted to go, and she looked up at him as they walked away from the bloodthirsty relics of old Hawaii. Kai believed in the ways of the old

74

Hawaiians, obviously.

'You would like to go to a party, wouldn't you?' he asked, catching her eye, and Kate pulled a face.

'Do I have any choice?' she countered.

'Sure you do,' Kai told her, and his teeth flashed like a white beam across that dark, savage face, 'but I don't think you'll turn it down, will you? For one thing because you'd like to see something of the high life for a change, and for another——' Kate met his eyes challengingly and he chuckled, 'you can't wait to see what Marjie Van Koren looks like!'

'I don't *care* what Marjie Van Koren looks like!' Kate denied forcefully. 'Why should I?'

That dark, unfathomable look was in his eyes again when he looked down at her and the hand under her arm squeezed hard into her soft skin, drawing her against the warmth of his body, setting her pulses racing wildly. 'Because Clara thinks I'm going to marry her little girl,' he said, and laughed, as if the idea was too ludicrous even to contemplate.

The moment she mentioned the prospect of going to the ball to Calvin he blinked in such surprise that Kate wondered just how important the apparently popular Belle Kildair was in island society. 'She actually asked you to her annual ball?' he asked, and Kate shook her head.

'Not personally, no,' she said. 'Kai simply said he was bringing me.' She looked up at Calvin, suddenly anxious as a new possibility entered her head. 'You don't suppose I'll be taken for a gate-

75

crasher, do you, Cal?' she asked. 'I'd hate that!'

'Oh, you'll have no trouble if you're with him,' Calvin told her bitterly. 'All doors are open to Kai Fernandez!'

'Oh?' Kate was thoroughly intrigued and Calvin's envy, although he couldn't have realised it, made her even more intrigued. 'Why's that?'

'His art!' Calvin jeered harshly. 'They say he's good, I wouldn't know, but the élite round here seem to think he's the greatest thing since Rembrandt!'

'I didn't realise that!' It was a new and interesting revelation, and she considered it as she walked along the edge of the surf with Calvin's hand holding hers so tightly he might almost have feared she meant to walk off and leave him.

He wore no jacket today, but a pale blue shirt and smart grey trousers gave him the customary air of formality that was part and parcel of his character. The open neck of his shirt was discreetly buttoned almost to the top and he suggested nothing so much as a city business man taking a lunchtime stroll, so that Kate was given to wondering, not for the first time, if there had ever been two such very different men so closely connected with one old man.

'He did that thing of the old man that hangs on the stair,' Calvin told her, and Kate looked up in surprise.

'That portrait?' she asked, and he nodded. 'But that's good—it's incredibly good!'

'You too!' Calvin said gloomily. 'Everyone says how good he is, no wonder he's so swelled-headed!'

76

'Oh, Cal!' She squeezed his fingers and smiled up at him encouragingly. 'You sound as if you're jealous of him, and you really have no need to be.'

'Don't I?' He turned and looked at her for a moment without speaking, his grey eyes going slowly over her features as if the fascination of them never palled. 'He's already taken you to the Bishop Museum and now he's taking you to one of the biggest social events of the year. Maybe I don't have the right kind of appeal or something, but I can't help feeling that I'm losing out fast to Kai Fernandez!'

'Oh, you're doing nothing of the sort!' Kate denied firmly. She liked Calvin a lot and she would have given quite a lot to have the choice of being taken to Mrs. Kildair's important party by him, but she couldn't quite see why she should miss the event because Calvin was jealous, although his jealousy was very flattering. 'You wouldn't want me to miss it, would you?' she asked, and he looked at her in such a way that she realised with a start that was exactly what he would like.

'I suppose you're looking forward to going?' he suggested, and gave her no time to answer. 'No, of course, you don't want to miss it, Kate, I wouldn't dream of suggesting you should!'

They once more walked in silence, and Kate thought suddenly how familiar the scene had become in just a short time. The surf, the sun-warmed grittiness of the sand between her toes, even Calvin holding her hand as he was now. Hawaii was already beginning to feel like home to her, and yet Kai would never have her anything but *malihini*—a stranger.

'Do you know Marjie Van Koren?' she asked suddenly, and without quite knowing why the name had come into her mind. 'We met Mrs. Van Koren in the museum,' she explained when he looked surprised. 'In fact it was she who issued the invitation from Mrs. Kildair—though only to Kai, of course.'

'Ghastly woman!' Calvin said with surprising vehemence. 'A real social climber, but a successful one!'

'Kai didn't seem to like her much either,' Kate told him, and he laughed shortly.

'She's a friend of his mother's,' he informed her. 'Or at least an acquaintance, I don't think she has any friends. I wish Fernandez *would* marry that awful daughter of hers, then maybe he'd move out of the beach house!'

'Is she awful?'

He pursed his lips, then rather surprisingly smiled, a small rueful smile. 'I guess not, not really,' he admitted. 'But she's not my type at all! Maybe she's Fernandez' type, almost anything in skirts *is*, though they'll be disappointed if they expect him to marry her!'

'You don't think he will?' Kate asked, and again he laughed shortly.

'Why should he marry? He's just like the old man and he'll——' He stopped hastily and looked at her with anxious eyes, as if he had just realised who he was speaking to so frankly. 'Oh, Kate, I'm sorry!'

She swung her free hand beside her carelessly, kicking at the warm sand as she walked and not looking at him. 'You don't have to be,' she told him with studied carelessness. 'I'm beginning to realise that I knew even less about my Great-Uncle Charles Wilmot than I thought I did.' She laughed uneasily, reluctant to admit the fact. 'I think he must have been quite a—a rip!'

'He was a good-hearted old man,' Calvin said seriously. 'I liked him, Kate, no matter if he did——' He shook his head. 'Well, that doesn't matter now. He enjoyed life and he liked wine, women and song, even when he was past eighty he liked to sit in the bars in town and watch it all happening around him. That's how come he left that five hundred dollars to the taxi driver—he used to drive them home sometimes.'

'Uncle Charles and Kai?' He nodded. 'And Freddie Leong drove them when Kai was drunk?' she suggested quietly.

He shrugged. 'I guess so, sometimes. I don't know.'

Kate took a moment to consider, to go over the words in her mind before she dared say them, and in view of her visit to the museum and all she had learned about Kai she wondered if she had any grounds for saying them at all. 'They're—they were quite a lot alike, weren't they?' she ventured.

'In some ways I suppose they were,' Calvin agreed, and it was obvious that he read nothing into her question except the obvious meaning, so that she said nothing more—especially about the possibility of there being very personal reasons for the likeness. It was much easier and more comforting to remember that Kai had said nothing about

79

having English blood in his veins, only that his mother was Welsh.

By mutual consent they turned back and began the stroll back along the same stretch of beach, saying little but lulled by the warm peace and quiet. The peace and quiet that Kai had said he needed to work, and she shook her head impatiently to rid herself of the persistent thought of Kai. It was always so difficult to put him completely out of mind and he was the most discomfiting ghost imaginable.

Climbing the wooden steps up to the house they still held hands, and as they paused on the doorstep Calvin turned her to face him gently, with his hands on her arms, his grey eyes looking down at her with an expression that sent little shivers of anticipation trickling along her spine.

'You're lovely, Kate,' he said softly. 'Very, very lovely, and I——' He stopped suddenly, his hands falling away, then he shrugged, looking uneasy and almost sheepish. 'No,' he said, shaking his head, 'I mustn't go on like that or you'll think the worst.'

'The worst?' Kate looked genuinely puzzled. 'I don't understand you, Cal.'

For several seconds he said nothing, instead he stood with his head bowed, looking at her mouth. 'You're a very rich girl now, Kate,' he reminded her quietly, 'and I half wish you weren't—not for your sake but for mine.'

'Cal, I don't——'

'Don't you see?' Calvin urged, taking her hands in his and squeezing her fingers hard as if to impress her with his sincerity. 'I'm beginning to fall in love with you, and you—well, you know how that'll look, don't you? I don't have to tell you what people like Kai Fernandez will say, and you could be forgiven for saying it yourself when you've just inherited close on half a million dollars!'

'Oh no!' Kate was anxious to reassure him, the more so because she saw his reasons only too well, and he was undoubtedly right about Kai's reaction. '*I* shan't think anything like that,' she denied, and laughed a little shakily as she shook her head. 'But I can't really believe you're falling in love already, Cal. Not so soon!'

Calvin bent his head and brushed his mouth across her forehead gently. 'I'm certain I am,' he insisted quietly.

CHAPTER FIVE

KATE seldom ventured into the sea alone, although she refused to admit that it was because her near drowning had made her nervous. The deep blue of the Pacific was quite unlike any other ocean, she felt, and the very surf that had almost swept her to oblivion was its greatest attraction.

Despite Calvin's contempt for it as nothing but showing off, Kate found the sight of a skilful surf-rider fascinating to watch and never tired of it. Much of Calvin's contempt, she suspected, stemmed from the fact that Kai was adept at the sport and he was not—jealousy, she recognised, was part of Calvin's make-up whether he realised it or not.

She made her way down the wooden steps from the house and stopped just before she reached the bottom, shading her eyes the better to watch the solitary figure skimming in on a huge comber, arms spread for balance, bending this way and that to steer the narrow board he rode on.

Muscular brown legs bent skilfully, guiding the board, and the gleaming bronze body balanced like a carved pagan god on the huge spume of spray that rolled him swiftly towards the sandy beach. It was Kai, she realised suddenly, and felt a strange curling sensation in her stomach as she watched him.

Presumably he believed himself unobserved, and he brought the surfboard ashore, shaking his black head and sending a shower of glistening drops shimmering around him. Showing off it might be to Calvin, but Kate found in it a stirring kind of beauty when the practitioner was as skilled as Kai.

For a moment seeing him there almost changed her mind about going in herself, but there was something irresistible about the shimmering blue surface that she could not deny, and she walked down the stretch of golden sand with her beach coat swinging open over a dark green bikini. She knew better than to get out of her depth now, but there was always Kai there if she did—somehow that thought was incredibly reassuring.

By the time she had walked the width of the beach and shed her beach coat, Kai was already in the water again, making for a particularly huge comber that came curling inshore at a terrific rate. Fascinated, she watched him from the water's edge, the foam running like creamy lace about her feet and ankles, and she held her breath when he chose exactly the right moment to stand upright on the narrow board and came skimming in towards her.

'Kai!'

Her cry was impulsive and she waved a hand to him, but had little hope of her voice carrying far enough to reach him. Poised like a bird on the crest of the huge wave, his golden brown body swayed as he exerted pressure on the speeding board, first one way and then the other, following the vagaries of the racing surf.

He was wearing what looked very much like a copy of the old traditional *malo*, the same type of brief loincloth he had shown her in the museum,

83

its gaudy colours in startling contrast to his dark skin. He looked, Kate thought a little breathlessly, very much as those early Hawaiians must have looked to Captain Cook or the early missionaries—dark, proud and excitingly savage.

She caught the sudden gleam of white teeth and realised he had seen her when he raised one hand in a gesture that threatened to overbalance him, and she put both hands to her mouth while she watched, unable to restrain a smile at the prospect. Kai, however, was much too experienced to be overthrown and he recovered almost at once to come skimming safely into the shallows as she herself took to the water.

She would never be able to emulate his skill on the surfboard, but she could enjoy the pleasure of swimming in the same warm sparkling sea, and she moved her arms lazily as she went out a little deeper. It was always so effortless swimming in this ocean, and she invariably felt a pleasant sense of lethargy.

'Kate!' Kai was behind her suddenly, swimming without the surfboard, his powerful arms bringing him swiftly alongside, and she tossed the clinging wetness of her hair from her face as she turned to look at him. 'I'll race you,' he challenged, but she laughingly shook her head. Against his speed and skill she had no chance at all.

'I'd be lost before I started,' she told him. 'You're much too good for me!'

'You don't know what you can do until you try!' Kai told her, his smile gleaming in that dark, primitive face. Something about him always seemed to be challenging her and she found it infinitely disturbing.

'I know my limits,' she said, and he merely smiled that time, making no comment.

She carefully stayed out of reach of the combers and swam at a leisurely pace in the warm, silky water, while Kai swam alongside, glancing at her every now and then with his dark expressive eyes. Then suddenly he was no longer there, and Kate blinked at the spot where a moment before his dark head had been, glistening jet black in the sun.

'Kai!' It was ridiculous, of course, to suppose he could have come to any harm in the shallows, but suddenly her heart was thudding at her ribs anxiously and she tried to see around her, seeking some sign of him close by. 'Kai! Where are you?'

He bobbed up as suddenly as he had disappeared, a few feet in front of her, and she frowned at him reproachfully. 'You should try swimming under the water,' he told her. 'Come on, Kate, try it!'

'No, thank you!' Still smarting from his casual lack of consideration, she tossed back her hair and used her legs and arms to keep her lazily afloat while she looked at him reproachfully. 'I wondered what on earth had happened to you,' she told him, and he looked briefly surprised, then, as if he found it too fanciful to be true, he laughed.

'You surely didn't think I could drown, did you?' he asked. 'Oh, Kate, you crazy little nut— how could I?'

'Because you're human!' Kate retorted sharply, annoyed because he found her concern for him amusing.

'Exactly,' Kai agreed, turning her argument to his own advantage. 'So if I can swim under water, you can—you'd like it, I promise.'

'I've no desire to drown just for the sake of showing off,' Kate told him, and he laughed again, his dark eyes glittering at her across the sparkling surface of the water.

'Is that what you think I'm doing?' he asked. 'Showing off?'

'Maybe not,' Kate allowed on second thoughts. 'But you swim like a fish, you've been swimming in these waters all your life, I haven't. You might swim like a—a native pearl diver, but I'm only a *malihini*, remember!'

Kai seemed to find that amusing, for she noticed a wolfish smile on his wide mouth that sent her heart fluttering nervously. 'You've been seeing too many old movies,' he told her, as soft-voiced as their environment allowed. 'But if you really wanted me to I could probably come up with a pearl for you in time.'

She would have protested, but he dived again immediately, swiftly and gracefully, a sleek dark shape through the shimmering water. Kate watched him, regretting, once again, that her tongue had run away with her and wishing she could find a reason for her constant desire to score off him.

It was fascinating to watch him, swimming as smoothly and easily as a great fish, and the desire to join him was irresistible suddenly. Briefly she felt a flicker of fear at the thought of plunging underwater, but then she shook herself impatiently and plunged downwards.

Immediately she panicked. Afraid to open her eyes, she found the enforced blindess gave her a sense of being held down and unable to surface again, but when she opened her mouth to cry out she drew water not only into her nostrils but into her mouth too, and she felt herself choking helplessly, unable to either breathe or see.

Threshing about wildly, she felt as if her lungs would burst and her fright was so complete that she reached the surface without even realising she was there. Strong brown hands seized her suddenly and shook her gently, gripping her arms with a grip that was at once both painful and reassuring.

'Kate?' Kai still held her, his hands hard on her soft skin, the warm, strong reassurance of his body pressing her close until her shivering panic died. 'Are you all right?'

Kate nodded, not trusting herself to speak, and he drew her towards him, closer still, one arm about her shoulders, the other still supporting her. Instinctively she laid her head on the smooth wetness of his shoulder while he stroked her hair and pressed his face to her brow.

'Must you plunge in at the deep end?' he asked against her ear, and Kate did nothing but nod her head slightly. 'What were you trying to do?' Kai asked, and she looked up at last, her eyes curiously bright and anxious.

'I—you said I should try swimming under the water,' she reminded him, and he shook his head, showering her with drops of water from the thick swathe of hair across his brow.

'But not without some help,' he told her. 'You didn't even hold your breath, did you?'

'No.' She made the admission reluctantly, and he laughed.

'No wonder you almost drowned yourself,' he told her. 'You can't swim without air under water any more than you can on the surface! What were you trying to prove, Kate?'

'Nothing,' Kate said through quivering lips. 'Nothing at all!' She felt too relieved to even object to his laughter and they swam side by side back to the beach. When they stood calf-deep in the water with the waves breaking around their legs Kai brought them to a halt, turning her towards him and trembling like a leaf when she tried to meet his gaze. 'I'm—I'm sorry for what I said, Kai,' she told him huskily. 'I mean about——'

'About me diving for pearls?' Kai asked with embarrassing frankness. His dark features glistened with sea water and he had that same primitive golden look that she remembered from the last time he had fished her from the sea. 'Oh, I guess you just wanted to get under my skin, didn't you, Kate?'

'No!' she denied hastily, then caught her breath. His hands on her arms held her firmly and she was tinglingly aware of the smooth bronzed body that just touched hers with an erotic, breathtaking contact she could not avoid. 'I—I don't really know what I meant,' she confessed. 'I'm sorry, Kai.'

'Truly sorry?'

Something in his voice made her look up at him

swiftly and his eyes were glittering darkly, like two flecks of jet in the sculpted features. The last time he had rescued her he had demanded that she show her gratitude, then, not content with her rather hesitant kiss, he had extracted his own payment in a way she recalled all too clearly. Being kissed by Kai, she remembered, was not an experience that was easily forgotten.

There was no mistaking the look in his eyes and she hesitated only briefly, but her heart was hammering wildly at her ribs as she tiptoed and, with her hands against the broad smoothness of his chest, lightly brushed his mouth with hers. 'I'm sorry, Kai,' she whispered. 'Thank you.'

He stood looking down at her with a bright, glistening look in his eyes that she found infinitely disturbing, then he slid his hands slowly from her arms and round her waist, drawing her to him, his mouth crooked into that slightly lopsided half smile. 'Thank *you*,' he said softly, and laughed.

Kate flushed, a warm bright colour in her cheeks as she glared at him angrily. She would have escaped, but the irresistible strength of his arms was drawing her closer until they moulded her to the glowing dampness of his body.

'You——'

She got no further than the one word of protest before the pressure of his mouth silenced her, his arms holding her close, crushing her hands between them so that she was bound and helpless as a baby. It was the same sensual, head-spinning experience as before and Kate, somewhere in the back of her mind, supposed she should have tried to do something about stopping it, but her own senses betrayed her.

His nearness, the contact of that vital, masculine strength with her own shivering uncertainty, was too much for her and she did nothing but close her eyes on a whole gamut of new sensations that she did not even try to understand.

It had seemed they were alone on that small sandy beach, but the voice that called out suddenly was not hers, and Kate opened her eyes swiftly, startled by its proximity. Pushing with her hands, she managed to break Kai's hold on her and stepped back, her eyes bright and frankly dazed as she turned and looked at the girl who stood on the sand, just at the water's edge.

'Kai?' She was small, dark and obviously *kamaaina*, for her skin was a beautiful glowing golden colour and her eyes as dark as Kai's own as she smiled at them. 'You forget me, cousin?' she asked him pertly when he looked at her, and Kai laughed, shaking his head.

Obviously he was much less disturbed by her appearance than Kate was, and he simply put an arm about Kate's shoulders and drew her along with him when he walked out of the water and up on to the sand.

Closer to, Kate realised, the girl could have been no more than about seventeen or eighteen and she had that slightly Oriental tilt to her dark eyes that quite a lot of Hawaiians had. Her face was smooth and doll-like and she seemed more amused than upset by what she had seen, so Kate assumed she was not one of Kai's female conquests—or if she was she was displaying a remarkable tolerance.

'Iolani,' Kai said with a smile as he put an arm round the girl, 'is a sort of cousin.' Briefly his dark eyes challenged Kate to comment, but when she showed no inclination to do so, he performed introductions with a gravity that she found rather suspect. 'Kate, this is Iolani Sikuyu Fernandez— Iolani, Miss Kate Wilmot.'

The pretty doll-like face smiled and the girl bobbed her head. 'Pleased to meet you, Miss Wilmot.' Her voice was soft and quiet and Kate thought she was quite enchanting, whoever she might be.

'Miss Fernandez.' She returned the girl's smile readily, but knowing she had witnessed those brief but disturbing few moments made Kate uneasy and she glanced at Kai through the thick concealment of her lashes. 'I—I think I'd better go back to the house and change into something dry,' she told him, and from his smile Kate knew he saw through her excuse.

He looked down at her, his dark eyes glistening and a hint of smile on his wide mouth. 'You don't have to mind Iolani,' he told her quietly, and Kate flushed.

'I mind *any*one seeing me in—in a situation like that, Kai,' she told him, her green eyes reproachful. 'It's likely to give quite the wrong impression!'

'Is it?' He was laughing at her, she felt sure of it, and it made her angry to think he found her reticence a cause for amusement. 'Aren't you being just a bit prissy, Kate?' he asked softly, and she curled her hands tightly in her palms.

Her heart was hammering loud and hard at her

91

ribs, and she wished she had never succumbed to the temptation to go swimming at the same time as Kai was there. Things so easily got out of hand when he was around, and she felt she was rapidly being cornered into admitting she was prissy now.

'Maybe I am,' she retorted. 'But I'm *malihini*, remember, not—what you call yourself!'

'Kate——'

'I'm glad to have met you, Miss Fernandez,' she told the girl, and eased herself out of Kai's light hold on her arm. 'Maybe I'll see you again.'

'Maybe,' Iolani Fernandez agreed, and looked up at Kai as if the whole situation puzzled her. '*Aloha!*' she said.

Kate acknowledged the expression with a brief nod and a smile and bent to pick up her beach coat. '*Aloha*,' she said a little self-consciously, and carefully avoided looking at Kai as she turned to walk back to the steps. She could not easily face that half-amused look in his eyes again, not when she thought of how she had responded to his kissing her.

Half way up the wooden stairway to the house she turned briefly and looked down to where Kai's beach house nestled among its riot of blossoming trees and shrubs. Just disappearing among the surrounding vegetation were Kai and his so-called cousin and as she watched them their laughter reached her, flattened by the distance and the open air, but unmistakable nevertheless.

Kai had one arm about Iolani Fernandez' slim shoulders and her head rested against him, and just as Kate turned away he bent his head and kissed the girl's mouth with obvious and uninhibited pleasure.

'She is supposed to be a cousin of some sort, I think,' Calvin said when Kate mentioned the girl to him, and it was obvious he found her curiosity puzzling. 'How did you come to meet her?' he added, and Kate shrugged.

'She came down to the beach when I was there.'

'I suppose she was visiting Fernandez,' Calvin guessed. 'He's got it made with that beach house to himself, he can do as he damned well pleases with no questions asked!'

'I had no intention of asking questions,' Kate told him a little sharply. 'I was much too embarrassed!'

'Embarrassed?' Calvin's grey eyes looked at her curiously and there was a small frown between his brows. Too late Kate saw that she had led herself into having some embarrassing explaining to do.

'I don't exactly mean embarrassed,' she amended, wishing she had never mentioned the girl at all. 'It was just that I——'

'Oh yes, I can guess,' Calvin interposed, nodding his head knowingly. 'Fernandez isn't exactly reticent about his little affairs. I guess you caught him with that girl kind of—well, in an awkward situation, huh?'

Kate's colour was bright in her cheeks and her eyes hastily avoided Calvin's narrow, disapproving grey ones. He could be scornfully sarcastic about Kai and Iolani Fernandez, but he probably wouldn't so easily accept that the girl involved had not been Iolani but Kate herself.

'It was an awkward situation,' she agreed readily enough, and decided to leave it with a half-truth rather than try to explain. Calvin's good-looking features were set in a tight-lipped look of distaste and she couldn't bear it if he were to direct that same distaste at her.

'I can imagine!' He laughed shortly and squeezed the fingers he held. 'I've seen that girl there before,' he went on, 'and frankly I don't altogether swallow that yarn about her being his uncle's adopted daughter. I've seen them together and he doesn't treat her the way I'd treat an adopted cousin!'

Kate, in her mind's eye, saw again the two slim brown bodies close together as they walked into the gardens of the beach house, and Kai's bent head as he kissed Iolani Fernandez' mouth. She had to admit that it was not the way Calvin would treat an adopted cousin, but she was not so sure about Kai —islanders were friendly and warm, she had already learned that much about them, and she had no doubt at all that a pretty girl was just that to Kai, whoever she was. Also her name *was* Fernandez, which seemed to suggest he had been telling the truth.

'You're not Kai,' she said quietly, and laughed a little uncertainly to cover her own doubts. 'And it really doesn't matter!'

It wasn't easy facing Kai again across that little table at dinner-time and Kate felt her heart thudding like a hammer at her ribs as she sat down facing him. Usually at dinner he affected a slightly more conventional mode of dress and this evening a bright turquoise shirt looked stunningly effective against the golden brown of his skin, its short sleeves exposing strong brown arms that reminded her irresistibly of how powerful they could be around her.

He said little for as long as it took for her to eat most of her meal, but Kate found her appetite lacking its usual relish because she had a strange sense of certainty that he was only waiting for them to end dinner before he raised some subject she would dislike.

What it was, she had no idea, but the certainty that there was something made her jumpy and uneasy. He gave her time enough to consume a delicious combination of icecream and mango, then poured out coffee for them both and leaned his elbows on the table, his cup between his hands.

'Cal came to see me,' he said without preliminary, and for several seconds Kate simply stared at him blankly.

'I—I don't understand,' she said at last. 'What has that to do with me?'

Kai sipped his coffee and his dark eyes looked at her steadily from above the rim of his cup. 'Quite a bit, I'd guess,' he told her quietly. 'Kate, what did you say to him about this morning?'

Kate caught her breath, her cheeks suddenly and betrayingly pink as she avoided his eyes. 'I—nothing,' she said, a little breathlessly. 'I—I simply told him I'd met Iolani Fernandez, that's all.'

'That's all?' One raised dark brow doubted it,

95

and Kate clutched her coffee cup with tight fingers. 'Come on, honey, what else did you say to make him mount that high horse of his and sail into me like a latter-day Don Quixote?'

'I said *nothing*, Kai!' She was so anxious for him to believe it that she gazed at him earnestly across the little table, her eyes wide and appealing.

He sipped his coffee again and savoured it for a moment before he looked at her again. 'Come on,' he said softly, 'you said more than nothing! Did you tell him I kissed you?'

Said like that it sounded so blunt and matter-of-fact and Kate cringed inwardly. 'No, I didn't,' she denied huskily. 'I just said I'd seen you with Miss Fernandez on the beach, which was quite true—I did.'

'You did,' Kai allowed, soft-voiced, his eyes glinting darkly. 'But what implication did you put on seeing Iolani there, Kate? That's what interests me!'

'I put no implication at all on anything!' Kate declared, her voice rising as she tried to guess what on earth Calvin could have done after he left her. 'What on earth are you talking about, Kai?'

'You don't know?' he countered, and she shook her head.

'Cal—Cal knew about Iolani,' she told him. 'He said he'd seen her there before.'

'It's possible,' Kai allowed easily. 'Iolani's quite a waterbaby, like most Hawaiians—so what did he gather from that? That I was making the most of my chances?'

Kate did not look up, she stared instead at her

empty plate and her hands moved restlessly, stirring her already stirred coffee, shifting her dessert spoon from one side of the plate to the other. 'Aren't you?' she asked huskily, and let out a small cry of surprise when a large hand fastened like a vice around her left wrist.

'So it *was* you behind it,' Kai said, his voice barely more than a whisper, and he held her wrist for several seconds before suddenly releasing it as if the touch of her repelled him. 'I guess you'd like to see me thrown out of the beach house, wouldn't you, Kate? Then you won't have to put up with having meals in my company!'

Kate stared at him, her eyes wide and disbelieving, one hand rubbing absently at her wrist. 'Thrown out?' she breathed. 'Oh no, Kai!'

His dark eyes held hers, glittering darkly below drawn brows. 'You didn't know?' he asked, and immediately shook his head in answer to his own question. 'No, I guess you didn't either.'

'I had no idea he had anything like that in mind at all,' she said. 'I—I'm sure you must have misunderstood him, Kai.'

He was shaking his head, firmly convinced he was right. 'He came and told me that I'd better think about finding some other place to live,' he said quietly. 'Since two of the beneficiaries were in agreement it was all he needed, he told me, to get me out.' He looked at her steadily for several seconds and Kate bore the scrutiny with her eyes downcast. 'I had you figured for the reason,' he said soft-voiced. 'I guess I had you wrong, Kate.'

'I wouldn't turn you out of the beach house,'

Kate told him. 'You have as much right there as anyone, Uncle Charles let you live there.'

'But it belongs equally to you and Cal too now,' Kai reminded her. 'You *could* have me thrown out on my ear, Kate, if that's what you want.'

'It isn't!'

Again that big hand reached across and touched her, but this time he did not grip her wrist, only covered her hand with his long gentle fingers. 'I'm glad I was wrong,' he said softly, and Kate drew in a sharp breath, drawing her hand back and shaking her head.

'What you do in the beach house is entirely your affair,' she told him, sounding quite appallingly breathless, and she looked up swiftly when he laughed. It was a deep, soft sound that trickled along her spine and curled her fingers into her palms.

'I guess you're right there, honey,' he said, and lowered one eyelid in a blatantly suggestive wink.

'Kai——'

'O.K.!' He raised both hands in the air in a gesture of surrender. 'I'm sorry I teased you!'

Kate looked at him for a moment with uncertain eyes, her head shaking slowly as she tried to solve the puzzle that was Kai Fernandez. 'I'll tell Calvin he doesn't have my support,' she promised in a quiet but not quite steady voice. 'I don't pretend to understand you, Kai, but I—I don't want to do anything that Uncle Charles wouldn't have approved of.'

Getting to his feet in one of those swift, effortless movements, Kai leaned across the width of the little table and pressed his mouth to hers gently. 'That's my girl!' he said, and Kate sat there wondering if she wouldn't have been wiser to have followed Calvin's lead and had her uneasy table companion removed to a safer distance.

CHAPTER SIX

It was hotter than Kate had known it so far and she had come much too far considering she was on foot. The Hawaiian climate was pleasant for strolling but did not lend itself to comfortable walking of a more energetic kind.

Her primary object in coming out at all had been to evade Kai should he return. They had had a brief clash of opinions at breakfast and she wanted to get away from the house on her own for a bit to cool down. Kai had disappeared soon afterwards and she had no idea where he was, but he was just as likely to appear again as not.

She found him an increasingly disturbing companion and sometimes wished she had let Calvin have his way about getting him out of the beach house. Calvin had been angry about her lack of support on that subject, although he had done his best to conceal it. His plan, once Kai was no longer in occupation, had been to sell the property or rent it, and she suspected his mother was firmly behind him in the idea. She had probably even suggested it.

Disturbing as she found Kai, however, she simply could not bring herself to drive him out of the place he regarded as his home. Perhaps Iolani Fernandez was his adopted cousin, or perhaps Calvin was right in his suspicions and the girl was merely one of Kai's casual affairs, but either way, Kate told herself, it was no concern of hers, and island customs in such matters were much more free and easy than elsewhere.

She shrugged her shoulders impatiently and tried to put both Calvin and Kai out of her mind. She was under no obligation to either of them and as long as she kept it that way what either of them did was nothing to do with her.

It was quite a relief, when she thought about it, to have some time entirely to herself and she must make the most of it. She had nothing special in mind to do, so a short walk along the beach had seemed just the kind of escape she needed. She had not meant to come so far, but an upward path among the bushes had drawn her attention and somehow the urge to go just a little further had taken her on long after she should have turned back.

It was a path well hidden from below and above and it wound along the rocky face of the cliffs, offering fantastic views, but even using all the available shade she had spent a lot of time in the sun and as a result she felt unpleasantly hot and sticky, although the spot she now found herself in was more than worth the effort of getting there.

There were rock cliffs both above and below where she was walking and in places the feathery tops of the palm trees that grew almost to the water's edge were actually level with the path she was on. Breathing heavily from her exertions, she felt rather like one of the early explorers, isolated but filled with the anticipation of finding something new at every step.

The ocean, vast and shiny as blue enamel, glittered dazzlingly and the surf hurled huge curling rollers on to the beach where they broke and spread out into a pattern of creamy lace on the hot sand. The thought of the water was suddenly irresistible to her and it was with the idea of getting to it that she looked for ways down.

There were several accessible but precarious routes, but she was quite nimble enough to negotiate them, and a cluster of palms blocking her path along decided her. Between the ragged rocks there was a way down and she decided to take it, for it seemed to offer plenty of shade, a rough natural path that sloped steeply but was safe enough if she was careful.

She had gone a little more than half way down when she stopped, breathing heavily and more than ever conscious of the stickiness of her body after the exertion. Then suddenly, there in front of her and slightly to one side of the path she was taking, was an opening in the trees and bushes and through it glinted the reflection of water in a pool.

The pool was formed in a hollowed out rock and half hidden by the lushness of the vegetation. It was possibly fresh water since it was well above sea level still, and it was quite small, no more than fifteen feet across, she guessed, but it looked deep and cool and very inviting to Kate in her present state. Almost completely surrounded by a thick barrier of palms and the exotic vegetation the islands abounded in, it was fed from a narrow trickle that fell from the rocks above, and nothing had ever seemed more inviting or more welcome.

The cool, soft sound of the falling water, the deep green pool and the closely growing trees and bushes—nothing was ever more ready made for just such a need as hers, and it was completely private too. There was no one about and the highway was much too far above her for there to be any fear of being come upon unexpectedly. Hawaiians were not habitual walkers, and anyway no one else would surely be crazy enough to take a cliff-path walk in such conditions.

She could get to it quite easily by going down over the rocks and without hesitation she turned off through the opening and scrambled down until she stood at the very edge of the pool.

It took her only a few seconds to decide that having no swimsuit with her need not deter her at all in this very private place, and only an inborn sense of propriety insisted that she used the concealment of a beautiful red-flowered ohia tree as a dressing room. The sacred tree of the goddess Pele, according to Kai, it seemed an appropriate shelter somehow in the circumstances and its exquisite red pompom blossoms would make it easy for her to find it again, for it grew as a solitary specimen here and not in numbers as it did in its more usual habitat on the cool lowlands of the volcano.

Kate had the strangest sense of excitement as she took off her few clothes and slid into the cool water of the pool, as if she had suddenly changed from being Kate Wilmot into someone quite different. She had never felt more relaxed or less inhibited in her life and she liked the sensation.

Taking a moment to accustom herself to the

change of temperature, she trod water and smiled to herself, shaking back her long hair from her face and noticing with some pleasure how golden her skin had turned in the few weeks she had been in Hawaii. It was a new experience, swimming naked in such surroundings, and so far she was enjoying it—an almost sensual enjoyment that lent a shine to her eyes and a pleasant sense of lethargy to her limbs.

Leisurely she swam across the width of the rock pool to where the clear water tumbled down from the rocks above, and found a foothold immediately below it where she could stand only waist-high in the water. Lifting her arms, she let the coolness of it run down them and over her whole body, her hair thinned and darkened by it as she closed her eyes and tipped back her head to cool her face and forehead.

There was no sound but the chittering of a bird somewhere in the bushes and the soft splashing of the waterfall into the pool. The shush of the surf was barely heard through the screening trees and there was a sense of timelessness that was incredibly soothing so that she left the cool, soft water of the pool only reluctantly.

Standing for a second on the edge, she shook back her hair, sending a shower of drops into the air, and using her hands to rub away the worst of the water from her face. The bird in the bushes again chittered protestingly and she half turned to smile at its objection, but saw nothing of it. It was a secret, private place and no one would ever know she had been there—Kai especially must never know, for he would tease her unmercifully about it.

Mrs. Leith's unfriendly eyes held suspicion and distrust and she seemed to Kate to be eyeing her with even more malice than usual when she told her there was a telephone call for her. The call puzzled Kate, for she knew no one outside the house, except Calvin, and he would hardly be calling her yet, since he had only just left.

'Did they say who it was, Mrs. Leith?' she asked as she followed the stiff, unfriendly back of the housekeeper across the hall, and Mrs. Leith half turned before walking off towards the kitchen.

'Mrs. Kildair,' she said abruptly, and stalked off as if the very mention of the name was distasteful to her.

Kate, with no time to gather her senses, picked up the receiver and murmured a rather breathless 'hello' into it. She had no idea what she expected to hear, but the pleasant and friendly voice put most of her fears at rest for the moment and she sighed inwardly with relief.

'Miss Wilmot?' There was a pause while Kate acknowledged her identity, then followed a light laugh that sounded as if the caller was slightly embarrassed. 'I'm sorry to have left it this late to issue an invitation, Miss Wilmot,' Mrs. Kildair told her, 'but you must blame Kai for that! You're a friend of Kai's, I understand?'

It could have been her imagination, but Kate was ready to swear that Mrs. Kildair was at the moment primarily interested in knowing just who she was, and while she hesitated to claim actual friendship with Kai it seemed to need less explanation than anything else at the moment. 'Yes,' she said, after a brief pause, 'I'm quite friendly with him.'

'Ah!' The satisfaction in that pleasant voice seemed quite out of proportion to Kate, and she hoped Mrs. Kildair wasn't putting the wrong construction on things. 'Well, knowing Kai,' Mrs. Kildair went on, 'you'll realise why I've only just heard about your coming to my affair tomorrow night, Miss Wilmot. He phoned me only half an hour ago and told me he was bringing you!'

Kate bit her lip; it was obvious what had happened. Mrs. Kildair had anticipated Kai being Marjie Van Koren's partner for the evening and his promise to bring Kate had disrupted his hostess's plans. Seeing her social evening rapidly becoming no more than a broken promise Kate did what she could to ease her unwilling hostess's difficulty.

'It's quite all right, Mrs. Kildair,' she told her, trying to sound as if it couldn't have mattered less. 'I know it's awfully short notice and you weren't expecting me, I don't mind in the last if you can't——'

'Oh but, my dear, it's nothing at all like that!' Mrs. Kildair hastened to assure her. 'Please don't think that's why I rang you! I simply wanted to apologise for not sending you a formal invitation. I never know where I am with Kai—do any of us?—but I don't want you to think you're not welcome, far from it, my dear, I do *hope* you'll come!'

'I'd love to,' Kate told her sincerely. 'And thank

you, Mrs. Kildair.'

'I knew your uncle, of course,' her caller went on, and from the tone of her voice it was clear that she had cared for Charles Wilmot in the same way that Kai had—as a genuine friend. 'We all miss him terribly, of course,' Mrs. Kildair went on. 'He was such a wonderful old man.'

Kate, more sure of herself at last, responded to the tribute with much more warmth than she had to Mrs. Van Koren's coy insinuations. 'I never knew him,' she said, 'but he seems to have been very popular with most people.'

'Oh, he was!' Mrs. Kildair assured her. 'And I'm so much looking forward to meeting you tomorrow night, my dear—I know you'll enjoy yourself!'

'I'm sure I shall, Mrs. Kildair, thank you.'

'But of course you will with Kai,' her caller told her confidently, and Kate could find no answer to that. 'Make sure you get him here in good time, my dear,' she added, and laughed. 'Goodbye!'

Kate hung up the receiver with a vaguely absent look in her eyes and only brought herself back to earth when she became aware of Kai from the corner of her eye, coming down the stairs, barefooted and silent on the carpeted treads and looking as disreputable as ever among the fine furnishings of Hale Makai.

He wore his usual paint-stained trousers with a brightly patterned print shirt that he had not bothered to button and which revealed most of the broad bronzed smoothness of his chest, and Kate took a moment to wonder hazily why he always seemed to look so much more attractive dressed as he was now.

His dark eyes glistened with laughter as he came nearer and one black brow questioned her rather absent air. 'Kate?' He snapped his fingers in front of her face, and smiled at her frown of annoyance. 'You look like you're lost in a dream,' he told her.

'I've just been talking to Mrs. Kildair,' Kate said. 'You might have let her know before this that you were taking me to her house, Kai.'

He stood immediately in front of her, one hand running carelessly through his thick black hair as he studied her for a moment. 'Oh, Belle's used to me,' he said. 'She won't take any notice of me leaving it till the last minute, don't worry!'

'Why did you, Kai?'

He searched her face, seeking some reason for her insistence, she guessed. 'Does it matter?' he asked. 'I just did, that's all.'

'Hoping you could find an excuse not to take me?' Kate suggested shortly, and his eyes narrowed.

'Nothing so dramatic,' he said quietly. 'Why in heaven's name should I want to find an excuse not to take you? I asked you, didn't I?'

'On the spur of the moment, I suspect!' Kate said, not altogether convinced of her own argument. Somehow she had got herself on a runaway course that she could not halt. 'Maybe so that you didn't have to bother about Marjie Van Koren!'

'Oh, for heaven's sake, you little idiot, do you really believe that?' He looked at her for a moment, then laughed shortly and reached for her with both hands, gripping her arms tightly and giving her a brief shake. 'I don't have to make excuses to avoid people I don't like,' he told her. 'I simply don't bother with them—and make what you like of that!'

Kate's slightly dazed brain coped as best it could. He was more or less telling her that he didn't need to avoid partnering Marjie Van Koren for the evening, and that his asking her had been a genuine desire for her company. It was incredible how much she enjoyed the idea of that although she did her best to accept the fact calmly.

'I just thought——' she began, but another slight shake silenced her again and he smiled down at her ruefully.

'*Don't* think,' he advised. 'You're too pretty to think, especially when you can't do any better than that!' He turned her round and put a hand under her arm, taking her with him across the hall towards the front door. 'You do *want* to go to this clambake, don't you, Kate?' he asked.

That was something she could answer easily enough and she nodded, glancing up at him as she did so. 'Oh yes, of course I do,' she said. 'I'm looking forward to it—I've even bought a specially grand dress to go in.'

'A grand dress?' He frowned briefly, as if he disliked the idea. 'I hope you're not going to appear looking too grand, I shan't know you!'

'But you said it was a ball,' she protested as he took her across to the door, and Kai merely smiled then shrugged.

He brought them to a halt on the porch in front of the house, with its masses of fragrant blossoms twining heavy-headed almost into the door itself.

Leaning forward, his body pressed her against the cool stone wall of the porch as he faced her, one hand either side of her head, his face only inches from hers.

Close to, his dark eyes had tiny creases at their corners that she had failed to notice before, and they glittered like jet in the shadows of the porch as he looked down at her for a long breathless moment without saying a word. Then he brushed aside a stray wisp of hair from her neck with one long finger, its touch on her neck as sensual as a caress, and shivering through her like a cool breath of warning.

'You don't need a grand dress to be the belle of the ball,' he said softly.

His voice was quiet and huskily seductive and she dared not look up at him. Her legs were suddenly so alarmingly weak that she felt they must let her down at any moment as she fought the persuasion of that voice and the gentle, erotic touch on her neck. 'Kai——' She had no idea what she wanted to say, only that she had to break the trembling silence between them.

'Do you know this is the first time I've ever actually taken anyone with me?' he asked softly, and she shook her head, much too breathless to speak. 'Not,' he added with a raised brow and a hint of smile, 'that I usually spend the evening in the corner as a wallflower, don't get me wrong, but it's bound to cause a few raised brows when I walk in with you and I thought I'd better warn you in advance.'

'You—you mean people might—comment?'

Kate asked huskily, and he studied her closely for a second, his gaze on her mouth.

'Do you mind?' he asked, and Kate shook her head.

He leaned towards her, the weight of his body forcing her back against the wall, and his mouth pressed hers, slowly and lingeringly until she felt her lips part. Her heart was pounding so hard against her side that she breathed as unevenly as a runner who has almost reached the limits of his endurance.

She put up her hands instinctively and placed them against his chest, not really pushing him away, but keeping him at enough distance to make sure he did not kiss her again, and he stood like that for several seconds. Then he smiled suddenly and shook his head. 'You don't really trust me, do you, Kate?' he asked softly, and she looked up swiftly, not sure what her feelings were at the moment.

'I—I don't know enough about you to decide what I feel,' she said in a small, shaky voice, and Kai laughed.

'Still curious!' he teased, his laughter blowing warmly on her face. 'Who am I? *What* am I? Poor little Kate! You're so curious and yet you never ask questions, do you?' He laughed again, tipping back his head and exposing the length of a strong brown throat and neck, while Kate's fingers curled into her palms in a reaction she did not fully understand.

'I know you're the most in*furi*ating man I've ever met!' she retorted defensively. She was still trembling like a leaf and she hated the idea of his realising it, so she pushed him away and ducked under his arm, standing immediately behind him, until he turned and faced her again.

'And you'd much rather Cal Morton was taking you to Belle's party tomorrow night,' he guessed, then shook his head. 'So would he, honey, I *know*!' he told her. 'But Cal's tried breaking into high society before—his face just doesn't fit, Kate.'

'Who says so?' Kate demanded, incensed on Calvin's behalf because she suspected snobbery.

'Well, not me!' Kai declared with a hint of anger. 'I don't care one way or the other!'

'Is it because he was my uncle's secretary?' she insisted. 'Isn't he good enough for them?'

Kai said nothing for a moment, but his eyes were bright and they glittered with something that made her shiver, as if he was trying hard not to speak out and make matters worse. Then he shook his head. 'You don't know enough about the islands to talk that way, Kate,' he said quietly. 'What a man is isn't important, but the way he—well, certain things matter, especially to friends, and I guess in this case Cal bears the brunt of something that isn't really his fault at all, but his mother's.'

'Mrs. Leith?' Kate frowned at him curiously, and he rubbed a hand over the back of his head, his own black brows drawn into a frown. He already regretted having said as much as he had, she thought, and his next words confirmed it.

'If you want to know the details, you'd better ask Cal,' he told her, and she shook her head firmly.

'Kai, you know I can't do that!'

He smiled ruefully. 'And neither can I, honey!'

'You could tell me why Cal isn't just as acceptable as you are,' Kate insisted. 'Why shouldn't he be? He was as close to my uncle as you were, and you've both inherited under his will! What makes Cal less acceptable than you? Tell me, Kai!'

'No, Kate!'

He sounded quite adamant, and she knew that if she wanted to know badly enough, she would have to ask Calvin himself, as Kai said, but she could no more question Calvin about himself than she could enquire too closely into Kai's background. There was so much she wanted to know, and no one she could possibly ask, and she sighed as she pursed her bottom lip in vexation while Kai shook his head slowly over her dilemma and was no help at all.

Calvin, despite the fact that he seemed to have integrated quite well into island life, still had a certain reticence about accepting the multi-racial Hawaiian society that most people automatically took in their stride. He was very conservative, and Kate guessed the views he held were to quite a large extent instilled by his mother's outlook.

Kate glanced up at him surreptitiously as they walked along the beach and tried to see what it was that prevented him from being as devastatingly attractive as Kai was. He was far better looking, there was no denying that, and he was charming, his manners were faultless and he never failed to do just the right thing when he was with her, and yet——

Maybe it was that earthy, almost savage sensuality that made Kai so much more disturbing, but something denied the same irresistible attraction to Calvin and she regretted it more each time she was with him. She would have been happy to fall in love with Calvin, and despite the prospect of having Mrs. Leith as a mother-in-law, she thought he would have made a good husband, whereas Kai was the last person in the world that any girl in her right mind would expect to settle down with.

Calvin turned and looked at her, drawn by the intensity of her gaze, and he smiled. 'What are you thinking about?' he asked, his fingers squeezing hers lightly, and Kate gave him a swift, teasing look through her lashes as she replied.

'You, as a matter of fact,' she told him.

'Truly?' He tucked her arm under his, still holding on to her hand, and his grey eyes smiled down at her. 'Then I won't interrupt you,' he said. 'Go right ahead and think about me, as long as it's flattering!'

'It is!' she admitted, and laughed. 'But don't get too inflated with the idea!'

'Kate!' He brought them to a standstill on the golden sand, turning her to face him and holding her arms with his long, firm hands as he looked down at her. 'You know how I feel about you,' he said quietly, and Kate instinctively shook her head, wondering what she had precipitated by making that facetious remark.

'Please don't, Cal,' she begged softly, hating to hurt him. 'I—I don't want to sound heartless, and that's what you'll think me if I tell you again how short a time it's been since I met you.'

'It's over a month,' Calvin reminded her. 'Not

such a short time, surely, Kate.'

'But it's not long enough to decide that you love me,' Kate insisted gently. 'It really isn't, Cal.'

He said nothing for several minutes, walking beside her with his hand holding hers again and a stiffness in his manner that communicated itself to her. 'How long will it take you to make up your mind about me?' he asked, after a few minutes of silence, and Kate looked up at him curiously.

'Oh, Cal,' she said softly, 'how can I answer a question like that?'

'It didn't take me long to decide how I felt about you,' he said quietly. 'But then you don't have the competition I have, do you?'

Kate glanced up hastily, foreseeing the direction he was taking and unwilling to have Kai brought into it in any capacity at all. 'I don't know how many other girls you know,' she told him. 'Quite a few, surely, you're a very good-looking man, Cal, and I wouldn't expect you to be a—a monk. I don't know what competition I've got!'

'Of course I'm not a monk,' he confirmed abruptly. 'But I never felt this way about anyone before, Kate, and I sometimes wish I was a smooth-talking operator like Fernandez!' Once more he brought them to a halt and spun her round to face him, his grey eyes bright with desperation as he looked down at her. 'Maybe I should take a leaf out of his book,' he said harshly, 'and just *take* what I want!'

'Cal!'

He ignored her protest and pulled her into his arms, his mouth set firmly. 'Why not?' he demanded. 'You didn't even try to get away when he kissed you on the beach that day! I can guess he figured it was a good opportunity to make you feel grateful to him after he made that dramatic rescue and then gave you the kiss of life, but like I said he makes the most of his opportunities and maybe I should do the same!'

'No, Cal, please!'

She put her hands to his chest, but her heart was beating more fast than normally and she was bound to respond to the sensation of being in his arms. He was undeniably attractive in his own more quiet way, but she was not yet ready to admit she found him irresistible.

'Kate!' He sought her mouth and pressed his lips hard on to hers, but the kiss was more a gesture of defiance, she felt, than a caress. 'I love you, Kate, I can't help myself!' he whispered, and the words were muffled by the thick silkiness of her hair as he buried his face in it, his mouth against the softness of her skin.

Kate stirred uneasily, for although she was indisputedly touched by the sense of urgency in his plea, she was also wary of being carried along by his persuasive coaxing into committing herself to something she would probably regret.

'Cal!' She pushed herself away from him, gently but insistently, and looked at him for a moment without speaking. Her heart was thudding hard at her ribs as she tried to find the right words without being too harsh. 'I—I'm sorry,' she said softly, and moved out of his arms, helpless to do anything about the hurt look in his eyes.

'Do I have no chance at all?' he asked after a second or two. He spoke in a quiet and peculiarly flat voice that somehow troubled her conscience, although there was little she could do about it.

'I didn't say that,' she denied softly. 'But it's too soon for me to—to commit myself, Cal—I'm sorry.'

He stood for a moment, looking so dejected that it was hard not to be tempted into relenting, no matter how rash it would have been. Instead she put a consoling hand on his arm, wanting him to know that she was more touched than he probably realised.

If only she could have fallen in love with Calvin, everything could have worked out well, but she felt she never could while that persistent niggle of doubt kept troubling her. She knew so little about him and somewhere at the back of her mind she kept hearing Kai's voice suggesting that she ask Calvin himself about his apparent unacceptability among some of her uncle's more reputable friends. But like so many things lately—it was easier to say than to do.

CHAPTER SEVEN

KATE was ready quite early the following evening, and a quite sickening sense of excitement curled in her stomach as she took yet another look at herself in the long mirror. She had never had a dress as sophisticated as the one she now wore and she was very undecided whether or not she liked the new Kate Wilmot who looked out at her with dark and doubtful eyes.

The girl in the Honolulu store where she had bought the gown had said it suited her perfectly, but now that she actually came to wear it she was much less certain herself, and wished she could fall back on a less biassed view than the salesgirl's.

From Kai she had learned that Mrs. Kildair's annual ball was given in aid of various island charities, and like so many charity occasions it was attended by all the wealthiest and important people in the islands, as well as a sprinkling of less notable guests to provide a balance.

In the circumstances Kate had felt that a really expensive and glamorous dress was a necessity. It was beautiful, there was no denying that, but its undoubted sophistication sat rather uneasily on such young shoulders, and she was not at all at ease in it.

Designed on the lines of the *holoku*, the old Hawaiian court dress, it fitted her slim figure perfectly and its scooped neckline exposed her pale golden tanned neck and shoulders to advantage. But one of the things that worried her most was the fishtail train at the back. A train was difficult to handle without practice and she felt strangely clumsy in it when she tried to walk, although it looked every bit as grand as she had told Kai it was.

Experimenting, she walked up and down her bedroom once again and frowned over the result. If only there was someone she could consult, someone whose opinion she could ask before she finally decided. She was still trying to make up her mind when she heard a door open downstairs, and sighed in resignation. It was just like Kai, of course, to be early just because she needed more time to decide.

Shrugging resignedly at the long reflection of her unfamiliar self, she picked her purse from the bed and opened the door. There was no time for second thoughts now that Kai was waiting and the next hurdle was facing his approval or otherwise of the controversial dress.

She managed to walk the length of the landing without mishap, although the fitted skirt restricted her movements more than she realised, but when it came to walking downstairs she found it incredibly difficult carrying the train, and her heart was hammering so violently hard at her side that she felt quite breathless.

'You're early!' She made the accusation partly to conceal her nervousness and partly to hide the effect of his completely unfamiliar appearance.

It was the first time she had seen him in anything but casual or semi-casual clothes and she scarcely recognised him as the paint-stained, half-naked creature she was used to, except for those deep, dark unmistakable eyes that said so much and hid so much more. In some strange way he looked like an older version of himself and she was forced to recognise for the first time that he was probably as old as thirty-four or five instead of no more than her own or Calvin's age.

Black trousers hugged the length of his long legs smoothly and a dinner jacket looked dazzlingly white in contrast to his dusky skin and the thick blackness of his hair, which tonight was tidily groomed. A white shirt with a frilled front softened the severity of the suit and lent a romantic air that set off his strong, primitive-looking features in stunning contrast.

He did not reply to her accusation but stood looking at her as she came down the stairs, coping with the train as best she could and also with a quite breathtaking heartbeat that increased as she bore his scrutiny. Stopping before she reached the bottom of the stairs, she stood facing him, her head held defiantly high and a gleam of defiance in her green eyes that dared him to criticise.

'You don't like it!' She felt the colour flood hotly into her cheeks and half turned away before he could say anything, ready to go back and change. 'Maybe it's as well you are early,' she told him, 'I'll have time to put on something else!'

'Kate!'

His call made her spin round again so hastily that she almost lost her balance, only recovering by hanging on to the balustrade tightly. His eyes moved over her inch by inch and she shivered as she stood there, her head high, but there was nothing critical in his appraisal that she could see, and her heart was clamouring wildly in her breast.

'I look all wrong!' she said breathlessly, before he could comment, and he shook his head, a hint of smile on his mouth as he looked up at her. 'I—I know I do!' she insisted.

'You look magnificent!' Kai said softly. 'Stunningly beautiful and elegant, but——' He shook his head slowly, as if in regret. 'You're not Kate, not like that! The woman you're trying to be now will develop naturally in about another ten years' time, but don't try to rush the process, honey, it's such a waste!'

'You—you'd rather I changed?' Kate was unsure whether to be disappointed or not that he shared her view, but he was looking at her in a way that disturbed her more than she cared to admit.

'Something simple,' he said softly at last. 'Something that makes you look soft and beautiful and much too young for me to be taking out!'

'That's silly!' Her voice sounded breathless and she could feel her legs trembling in the most alarming way as she stood there on the stairs looking down at him.

One black brow flicked upwards and he half smiled. 'Is it?' he asked.

'Kai——'

'You have five minutes,' he told her, glancing at his wristwatch. 'It shouldn't take you that long, honey, to change that dress and brush out your hair again.'

She put a protective hand to her newly styled

hair and protested, 'Oh no, I can't undo——'

'You can if you want to go to this clambake,' Kai told her firmly, and laughed. 'Come on, honey, chop-chop!'

It took a little longer than five minutes for her to put on a simple, ankle-length dress of white voile with a demurely high neck and cut away to show off her arms and the smoothness of her shoulders, but she had to admit that she felt much more at ease than in her grand ball gown. She hesitated about disturbing her newly styled hair, but decided it would look more suitable with her present dress if it was worn loose, so she brushed it out, as Kai has suggested.

When she came downstairs again Kai was waiting in the hall still, and he looked up when she appeared, his dark eyes glinting with approval, as he came forward to hand her down the last few steps with unexpected gallantry.

'Nani!' he said softly as he took her hand and steered her towards the door, and Kate remembered that meant beautiful—perhaps it had been worth changing, she decided.

Mrs. Kildair's home was more grand even than Kate could have anticipated, and she felt nervous to the point of panic as she got out of the car and climbed the steps to the open doors supported by Kai's arm. The house seemed to be already full of people when they arrived, and the sound of their voices along with the sound of an orchestra reached them even before they left the car.

Kate's legs were trembling and she clung to Kai's

arm more tightly than she realised, apparently, for he turned and looked down at her as they went into the house, smiling enquiringly. 'Are you nervous?' he asked, and Kate nodded.

'Yes, of course I am,' she told him. 'I'm not used to these—clambakes, as you call it. I only hope you don't live to regret having brought me—if you do it'll be your own fault for bringing me!'

Kai laughed softly as they walked into a vast and crowded room whose milling occupants spilled over into the gardens beyond via some wide open sliding glass doors. 'You're being aggressive, Kate,' he told her, 'and that means you're on the defensive!'

'I'm not,' Kate denied swiftly, 'but I——'

'You are,' Kai insisted, and his strong fingers took her hand and squeezed hard. 'You don't have to be, Kate. Just act naturally, you'll find everyone else does.'

Kate looked around her at the glittering collection of obviously wealthy women in their expensive gowns and jewellery and felt suddenly very small and nervous—far too much like Cinderella at the ball. 'They all look much too grand to behave other than impeccably,' she told him, and again he squeezed her fingers reassuringly.

'Nonsense!' His dark eyes glittered down at her challengingly and his wide mouth was touched with a hint of devilment that did strange and exciting things to her pulses. 'Take off your shoes if you feel like it, and dance on the lawn,' he advised. 'I probably shall, nobody'll mind!'

Kate giggled. It was sheer nervousness, of course,

but she felt a stirring excitement in her that owed
at least part of its existence to the nature of her
companion. Kai had the enviable and rare gift of
making outrageous suggestions sound like common
sense, and she already felt more at ease as she
turned to meet her hostess.

Belle Kildair was something of a surprise too; for
one thing she was much younger than Kate had
imagined her to be, although the expensive atten-
tions of both her dressmaker and her beautician
undoubtedly did a lot towards creating the impression. She was fairly tall and at first glance not unlike Mrs. Clara Van Koren, but the eyes were
kinder and the smile more friendly than coy as she
took both Kai's hands in hers and looked up at
him. She was undoubtedly a devoted admirer, but
she was much less cloyingly obvious about it.

'Kai!' she said, and tiptoed to plant a kiss firmly
on his mouth. 'You've been neglecting us all again
—I do *wish* you wouldn't hide yourself away in
that beach house, honey, we miss you!' Still holding on to one of his hands, she turned to Kate and
the blue eyes were both friendly and curious. 'Kate
Wilmot,' she said softly, and proffered a hand, en-
folding both Kate's in hers impulsively. 'And I
guess you're just about as pretty as your grand-
mama was, aren't you?'

'I'm like her,' Kate agreed with a smile, faintly
puzzled, and Belle Kildair laughed, squeezing her
hands.

'Oh, I heard all about it!' she told her. 'I heard
so much about Lizzie Ardon from Charlie that I
guess I know just about as much about her as her

family do!'

'Oh, I see!' It was touching, Kate thought suddenly, to think of the old man, so far from home, in self-imposed exile because he loved the girl his brother married, but unable to keep from talking about her to his friends.

'It was so romantic,' Mrs. Kildair insisted, 'and I was so *glad* he made that gesture at the last, honey, I really was!'

'So am I, Mrs. Kildair,' Kate told her with a smile. 'I wouldn't be here otherwise, and I'm enjoying myself enormously living in Hawaii.'

'But of course you are!' Swiftly the blue eyes flicked in Kai's direction, and Mrs. Kildair smiled knowingly. 'Who wouldn't—you lucky girl!' Before Kate had time to do more than rather dazedly shake her head to deny the implication, Mrs. Kildair squeezed her hands again and laughed. 'We must have a long talk some time about dear old Charlie,' she told her.

'I'd like that,' Kate said, and meant it. Anyone who had known her uncle was of interest to her, for she had a growing need to know more about the old man who had, by his generosity, changed her life completely.

A tall slim blonde girl was coming through the crowd on the dance floor and Kate felt her heart give a sudden lurch when she saw her, for she felt certain in her own mind that the girl was Marjie Van Koren, whose mother had earmarked Kai as her son-in-law. It was a meeting Kate had dreaded ever since she first heard of her, and she curled her hands tightly into her palms when their hostess turned and spoke to her, rather breathlessly, as if she found her arrival embarrassing.

'Marjie dear!' she said. 'Has Robert deserted you? Oh, that's too bad of him!'

'I deserted him, I guess!' It was obvious that sympathy was neither wanted nor needed, for Marjie Van Koren knew her own mind and her eyes were fixed firmly on Kai. Hard blue eyes, uncannily like her mother's, but set in a face that was at once beautiful and harsh, a warning clue to her identity. From the way she looked at Kai, one brow raised and a hint of thrust in her bottom lip, it might almost have indicated that she expected him to apologise for something. 'Hello, Kai,' she said quietly. 'How's your work going?'

If she expected him to be discomfited, however, she knew Kai less well than she imagined, for he merely smiled and, with one hand still beneath Kate's arm, squeezed her soft skin with his strong fingers, as if in reassurance. 'Fine, thanks,' he said quietly. 'You don't know Kate, do you?'

'I've heard the news,' Marjie Van Koren said flatly, making her lack of interest in the subject quite evident, but Kai ignored the snub and completed the introduction.

Kate's extended hand was barely touched by long, cool fingers and the look in the light blue eyes was chill enough to make her shiver inwardly. In one way Kate could sympathise with her, for it must be quite a blow to her pride to have Kai turn up at this very public affair with another girl, but she would make a very bad enemy, and Kate recognised it with some caution.

Mrs. Kildair's house did not overlook the sea as Hale Makai did, but it had a wonderful elevated view of the lights of Honolulu after dark, and Kate found it fascinating. Having danced with Kai for a good deal of the evening so far, she had eventually been abandoned, at her own request, while he partnered their hostess and Kate had taken the opportunity to come out into the garden and enjoy some fresh air.

The fragrance of the now familiar blossoms tickled her nose pleasantly as she walked down a winding, shrub-lined path that ended with a row of towering jacarandas standing like grey ghosts in the moonlight, their fern-like foliage fluttering against the night sky and the bell-shaped blue blossoms appearing darkly colourless without the benefit of sunlight.

She had been out longer than she intended, but the peace of the gardens was tempting and she granted herself another moment or two before going back. Beyond the jacarandas the bushes grew thicker and it was less easy to find a way through them so that she soon feared for the condition of her flimsy dress and turned back. But as she turned a faint whisper of movement reached her and she looked swiftly across in the direction it came from.

Apparently thinking themselves unnoticed, two figures stood in a small clearing, clearly identified by the bright moonlight, and Kate caught her breath when she recognised them. Marjie Van Koren's arms reached up as Kate watched, too startled to move, and wound themselves about Kai's neck, her mouth pressed to his and the darkness of his large hands like two inky patches on her light gown as he drew her closer.

Hesitating no longer, Kate turned swiftly and walked back to the shadow of the jacarandas before she even paused for breath, her breathing short and erratic, although she had not hurried unduly. Her hands were tightly curled and her face flushed as she coped with a quite unexpected surge of anger.

She stood there for several minutes, her brain in turmoil, yet unable to produce any sound reason why she should have been so affected. She walked up and down between the trees, trying to make herself see reason, and gradually, after some minutes, she relaxed. There was no reason, she told herself, why Kai shouldn't kiss his erstwhile girlfriend if he felt like it, after all he meant nothing to Kate nor she to him. It was completely unreasonable for her to be so upset by it.

A beautiful melia tree, stirred by the night breeze, touched her flushed cheek as she stood by it, and she absently broke one of the pale blossoms from its stem and held it to her face for a moment, savouring its incredible fragrance before impulsively tucking it behind her ear as she had seen the Hawaiian girls do.

There was nothing to stop her enjoying the rest of the evening as much as she had the earlier part, and if Kai wanted to change partners she was unlikely to be short of offers herself. The melia blossom tickled her cheek and she put up a hand to it, touching the cool velvety petals gently. Kai would find her gesture of tucking the flower into her hair another cause for amusement and he would probably tease her about it. Kai! She shrugged him impatiently from her thoughts and looked up at the huge bright silver moon—Kai was no different from what he had ever been, and she had no reason to suppose he ever would be!

'Kate?'

She turned swiftly, her heart thudding like a wild thing when she recognised his voice. A small, slim figure in the moonlight, looking as if she was poised for flight, with a pale blossom in her hair and her eyes wide and wary, she looked at him in silence.

His face was shadowed by the trees and it looked incredibly dark, with only the white gleam of his teeth to betray the fact that he was smiling. Heaven knew where Marjie Van Koren was now, but perhaps she had simply been suitably appeased and sent back to join the rest of the party. There was no limit to what Kai could achieve if he was just charming enough.

'Going native?' he asked softly, and Kate shrugged.

She would rather he had gone anywhere after he left Marjie Van Koren than come to her, for already her pulses were pounding wildly and her heart was fluttering at her ribs as if it sought to escape. It alarmed her to realise, in the few seconds he waited for her to answer, that she too was much too vulnerable to Kai's charm, and particularly in such a setting as this.

'It—it's a beautiful perfume,' she said in a voice she tried hard to steady.

Kai nodded, and coming a step closer he reached out and touched the blossom with his fingertips, the touch of his long, cool fingers against her flushed cheek sending a shiver through her body. 'It suits you,' he said. 'But then you're just made for all the romantic trimmings of Hawaii, aren't you, Kate? Old Charlie must have known it when he fixed for you to stay on here!'

'He probably guessed I'd like it,' said Kate, then caught her breath when a new and disturbing possibility came into her mind.

Her heart gave a lurch suddenly and for the first time since her arrival she really stopped to wonder just why Charles Wilmot *had* made that provision in his will about her staying on for at least a year in Hawaii.

She had never really looked for reasons before, but now, with Kai standing so close in that bright exotic garden, she felt a strange certainty that things were going just the way the old man had wanted them to. He had been fond of Kai and of her too, presumably, since he had left her the bulk of his fortune, so maybe—— She shook her head hastily to dismiss the idea as ludicrous, for surely he had known Kai better than that—Calvin was a less unlikely candidate for the role.

'He was a great believer in the institution of love and marriage,' Kai told her with a smile, and coming so soon after her own train of thought it startled her for a moment, although it was ridiculous to suppose his own thoughts ran along the same lines.

'Then—then why did he never marry?' she

asked, and Kai shook his head.

Thrusting both hands into the pockets of his trousers, he leaned back against one of the trees so that his dark features were even more inscrutable. 'I guess he never found anyone else who looked like his beloved Lizzie,' he said. 'But he never tired of trying to marry me off, he said it would do me good, and he was forever trying to find me a wife!'

'Like Marjie Van Koren?' Kate asked rashly, and to her surprise he laughed.

'Good grief, no!' he said. 'Charlie couldn't stand the Van Korens, though Clara would have married him quick enough if he'd asked her!'

'But surely *you* don't dislike the Van Korens,' Kate ventured, glancing at him through her lashes. 'Particularly Marjie!'

Kai said nothing for a moment and his eyes were luminously dark in the shadows, then he smiled, a brief gleam of white teeth in his dark face. 'So you *were* the little ghost who fled through the trees!' he said, and sounded more amused than annoyed at being seen kissing Marjie Van Koren. 'I thought it looked like you fluttering away through the bushes!'

'I'd no idea you were there,' Kate told him hastily, 'or I'd never have come down there.'

'No, I guess you wouldn't have.' He watched her for a few moments in silence while Kate stood in the moonlight, feeling strangely exposed and vulnerable. 'But you're mad about it, aren't you?' he suggested softly after a while and Kate drew a sharp breath to deny it.

'Why should I mind?' she asked as quietly as she

could. 'It doesn't concern me in any way, who you —you flirt with, Kai.'

'Hmm!' He watched her for a moment longer. 'You know, honey,' he said at last, 'I sometimes wonder if getting me married off and keeping you here wasn't somehow tied up in the old man's mind when he made that will.'

He sounded serious enough when he spoke, but then Kate heard him laughing softly and it made her quite unreasonably angry. She curled her hands tightly and looked at him with bright, defiant eyes. 'I don't think that's very likely,' she told him in a small breathless voice.

'No?' The single, softly spoken word had a ring of challenge that Kate was bound to respond to.

'For one thing,' she argued huskily, 'he had no way of knowing whether I'd even like you, let alone marry you, and second he must have known that you'd never stay interested in any girl long enough to marry her!'

'And third,' Kai interposed swiftly, 'you didn't know Charlie Wilmot any better than you know me!' His argument surprised her and Kate stared at him for a moment, her lips parted and her eyes wide and searching, trying to detect exactly what he meant. 'He was as devious as a whole crate of monkeys,' Kai insisted. 'He'd do it if he thought it would work—you didn't know him, Kate, I did!'

'So you keep reminding me!' Kate said shortly. 'But I—I don't *believe* my uncle's last thoughts were on matchmaking!'

It was difficult to be so adamant when her own thoughts had run in that direction only minutes

before, but she found it too discomfiting a proba-
bility to face. Kai, however, still leaned against the
tree with his hands in his pockets and he was smiling as he studied her. 'Ah, come on, Kate,' he said.
'Don't tell me the same thought's never entered
your pretty little head! What reason did you give
yourself for his wanting you to stay on here?'

Kate licked her lips anxiously. She felt rather as
if she had been cornered, but also strangely excited
and that was less easy to understand. 'I—I hadn't
even thought about it,' she told him, and he
laughed shortly.

'Do you know,' he said, 'I almost believe you!'

'I don't care whether you believe me or not!'
Kate declared. 'If Uncle Charles knew you as well
as you claim he did, then he must have known that
marriage was the last thing on *your* mind, whoever
he had in mind for you!'

He moved at last, easing himself away from the
tree with one smooth movement, taking his hands
from his pockets and brushing down his jacket as
he looked at her steadily. 'You know *so* much, don't
you, Kate?' he asked softly.

'I don't claim to——'

He silenced her with the sudden hard pressure of
his mouth over hers and she fought hard against
him for a moment, her hands pounding ineffectu-
ally at his chest. Marjie Van Koren might be
cajoled and persuaded by his kisses, but not Kate.
Then suddenly she wasn't fighting any more, but
yielding softly to the insistent pressure of his arms
and the fierce persuasion of his mouth, and he
pulled her even closer to the warm, sensual

strength of his body until she no longer had the strength or the will to resist.

'Kai——'

She spoke in a small, trembly voice that was scarcely recognisable as her own, and looked up to see the glittering jet blackness of his eyes looking at her with a curiously speculative expression. 'You know, it might just be a good idea to marry you,' he said softly, and kissed her mouth again lightly. 'You wouldn't say no, would you, Kate?'

'Kai, stop teasing me!'

She struggled free at last and stood facing him, her whole body trembling like a leaf and horribly unsure if he was serious or simply making a joke of the whole thing. His eyes looked deep and unfathomable and there was no way of knowing what was really going on behind those dark features.

'If you don't marry me, Cal Morton'll talk you into it sooner or later,' he told her bluntly. 'And I don't think Charles would have liked that at all, honey!'

Kate looked at him with bright, angry eyes and her hands were tightly curled at her sides, for she had never felt so helplessly unsure of herself in her life before. 'I could quite easily hate you,' she told him in a quavery voice, and firmly believed she could, in that moment. 'For your information, Cal loves me. He's told me so and——and I believe him!'

Kai flicked one black brow swiftly upwards and a hint of smile just touched his wide mouth for a moment. 'I guess he does,' he said quietly. 'You're a great catch, Kate honey—not only rich but beautiful too!'

Kate's reaction was swift and instinctive and her hand connected with the tanned smoothness of his cheek with more fury than she realised, making him shake his head in surprise. Then she took to her heels and ran back towards the house, flitting like a pale ghost between the perfumed trees.

'Kate!'

His voice followed her through the moonlit garden, but she did not slow down nor even turn around until she reached the sanctuary of the wide lawns where other people sat drinking at small tables under fairylit trees, or strolled around under the blossoms, talking together.

Her heart was pounding with unmerciful fury at her ribs and she knew her cheeks were flushed from running. The flower she had tucked into her hair was gone too, lost somewhere along her flight path, and she brushed back her hair as she walked back into the noisy, brightly lit room full of people.

Maybe she should not have slapped him as she had, but it was a reaction to a series of events and she made no excuse for her action. It had been a form of protest, an outlet of all the minor upheavals he had caused her during the evening and not just an objection on Calvin's behalf.

'Are you O.K., Kate dear?' Mrs. Kildair's kindly voice from just behind her made her spin round hastily, and she smiled.

'Yes, thank you, Mrs. Kildair.'

The blue eyes looked out through the garden door and it was evident what was going through her mind. 'I thought I saw Kai going out again to find you,' she said, then looked at Kate's flushed cheeks and the unnatural brightness of her eyes. 'Oh!' she said. 'Oh dear, you two haven't had a fight, have you?'

It seemed almost laughable suddenly when Kate thought of how stunned Kai had been when she slapped him. If she had stopped to think of possible consequences she would never have had the nerve to do it, but now, in some curious way it gave her a strange sense of exhilaration to remember it.

'We just had a slight—difference,' she admitted with a rueful smile, and Mrs. Kildair shook her head.

'I knew he was wrong to go out there with Marjie,' she said anxiously. 'I am so sorry, Kate dear!'

'Oh, please don't be,' Kate told her lightly, 'it had nothing to do with Miss Van Koren! We simply didn't see eye to eye about—well, about something very personal, and——' she laughed a little hysterically when she made the confession, 'I slapped him!'

'Oh, Kate!' Mrs. Kildair's elegant features looked shocked, but there was a deeper glow in her blue eyes that betrayed laughter, and after a mere second or two she put a hand to her mouth and laughed softly. 'Poor Kai,' she said in a half whisper. 'It must be quite a chastening experience for him! He'll be out for revenge, honey, you'd better watch out!'

Kate, still with that strange sense of exhilaration, shook her head, but nevertheless glanced behind her at the moonlit garden. 'Don't tell me there's some mysterious and bloodthirsty method of dealing with females who step out of line,' she said with a laugh. 'Kai's told me about the *old* Hawaiians—are the new breed just as ruthless?'

'It's a picture that Kai likes to encourage,' Mrs. Kildair told her with a smile. 'The idea of being thought of as a primitive islander appeals much more to his sense of the dramatic than simply saying he has a charming and respectable Portuguese/French father whose family have been here for about three generations now, and a lovely Welsh mother.'

'Portuguese and French?' Kate asked, feeling that even that combination was exotic enough to please most people, and Mrs. Kildair nodded.

'It's quite a common combination in the islands,' she said. 'But Kai's father looks rather less primitive than his son, mostly because Kai spends so much time in the sun he's tanned that gorgeous dark brown. Because he's so brilliant at his job no one minds that Kai lays on the wild islander act!'

'He's a good artist,' Kate agreed, and Mrs. Kildair nodded.

'He's brilliant,' she said. 'If he'd stuck to portraits he'd have made a fortune, but he's so independent he prefers to hide away in that beach house and paint anything he pleases—that's why he was so fond of Charlie Wilmot, I guess the old man understood him better than most of us do.'

'I see.' It had been so easy after all, Kate thought a little hazily. There was no mystery either about Kai's parentage or about his attachment to her uncle—he had simply been a friend who offered him a bolt-hole from the profitable but boring prospect of painting nothing but polite society portraits.

Mrs. Kildair's hand on her arm brought her back to earth suddenly and she followed the direction of her inclining head. 'I think you're about to be whisked away,' her hostess told her with a chuckle. 'Kai looks like he means business!'

'Oh, Mrs. Kildair——'

She would have followed her into the concealing crowd, but it was already too late. Mrs. Kildair had disappeared and Kai was striding towards her, his brows drawn together into a dark straight line above the glittering darkness of his eyes. In one big hand he carried, with curious gentleness, the blossom she had dropped, and he came towards her unhesitatingly.

Without a word he bent and tucked the melia flower into her hair above her left ear, his strong fingers brushing her cheek and sending little shivers of sensation over her whole body. 'That means you're spoken for,' he informed her in a firm, quiet voice. He drew her towards the dance floor, unresistingly, and his arms slid round her as he pulled her against the steely hardness of his body. 'Now dance,' he whispered harshly against her ear, 'before I change my mind and give you what you deserve!'

CHAPTER EIGHT

KATE woke up feeling quite incredibly light-hearted, and she lay for several minutes going over the events of last night in her mind. Her eyes wide open, she gazed up at the ornamental ceiling of her room where the sun already splashed shimmering gold patterns, reflecting the water in the pool outside.

What had at one time promised to be a disaster had turned out after all to be the most enjoyable evening she ever remembered. She had danced, mostly with Kai, until the very early hours, and drunk just a little too much, so he had informed her, though entirely without censure.

She had laughed a lot too because she had felt so lightheartedly happy with everything, and even Marjie Van Koren's envious blue eyes had done nothing to deter her. The evening had ended with her waltzing around the almost deserted floor with Kai while Mrs. Kildair chatted to some friends and smiled benevolently.

Coming home in the car with Kai they had said very little, but there had seemed no need for conversation and she had been content to simply put back her head on the comfortable cushion behind her and look out at the ocean and the moon, thinking how wonderful it would be to stay there for ever.

True, it had seemed something of an anti-climax

at the time when Kai had said goodnight with no more than a mere light, gentle kiss that only briefly warmed her mouth, and a long glittering look from those dark eyes that promised so much more. Her air of slightly tipsy excitement, she could see now, had probably made him realise that one of them should keep their feet firmly on the ground.

Stretching her arms above her head, she smiled and then pulled a face when she realised how late it was. Mrs. Leith was probably prickling with resentment with no one down to breakfast on time, unless of course Kai had a stronger constitution than she had and needed less sleep. Laughing as she got out of bed, she shook her head—even Kai would find it difficult to pacify Mrs. Leith.

A long leisurely bath refreshed her and she put on a pale green cotton dress over her swimsuit, then brushed her long hair vigorously until it shone—there was no need for elaborate preparations this morning.

The grand ball gown she had bought and then changed her mind about wearing still lay across a chair, and she shook her head over it. Kai was right, of course, it was too mature for her at the moment and the soft simplicity of the one that now lay across the foot of the bed was much more her style. Briefly she picked it up and held it against her, twirling round in front of the long mirror— her first plunge into society had been a definite success.

Coming down a few minutes later she walked into the long sunny room where the glass doors stood wide open to the balcony above the sea, and felt her heart fluttering when she saw Kai was already there.

Back in his more familiar garb this morning, he wore the paint-stained trousers with a gaudy shirt slung carelessly about his shoulders only. No doubt he was barefoot too, as he most often was, and she felt strangely shy suddenly at the prospect of an intimate breakfast with him at that small table.

He turned when she came in and got to his feet as he always did, his dark eyes brightly curious as ever. 'Good morning, Kate,' he said quietly, and she smiled.

'Good morning!'

'Quite recovered?' he asked as he sat down again, and Kate looked at him enquiringly.

'From the party?' she asked. 'Oh, I'm fine, thank you, are you?'

'Great!' His wide mouth twitched into a suggestion of a smile and his brows rose to the customary thick swathe of hair across his forehead. 'I wasn't flying quite so high last night,' he told her. 'I thought you might be feeling a little—thick-headed this morning.'

'Why on earth should I be? I wasn't drunk!' As always when she was on the defensive she sounded angry, and he smiled and shook his head at her.

'I didn't say you were drunk,' he denied. 'I merely said you were flying a little high, honey, and so you were. You were way up in the clouds!'

'Is that why you behaved with such gentlemanly restraint?' she retorted, and realised as she said it what kind of impression she could give.

Kai said nothing for a moment but poured himself more coffee and raised the cup to his lips before he answered, his eyes looking at her across its rim, bright, dark and unfathomable. 'I figured I was old enough not to take advantage of the situation,' he told her at last. 'I kept seeing old Charlie at my elbow and it kept me on the straight and narrow, but I was tempted, honey, believe me, only——' He shrugged his broad shoulders in a gesture that said it all. 'It wouldn't have been fair in the circumstances, Kate honey, you looked so—so childlike and trusting I just hadn't the heart!'

'You——' Kate's green eyes sparkled brightly in her flushed face and her hands curled tightly as she glared at him. 'How dare you make it sound as if I was—as if I meant——'

A black brow questioned her meaning and there was a glint of laughter in his eyes that stung her pride. 'Maybe I got you wrong,' he suggested softly, 'but it sounded to me like you were mad about something.'

'I'm mad about you talking to me as if I was just out of kindergarten!' Kate told him shortly. 'You haven't the right to talk to me like that!'

'I figured I had no rights at all,' Kai told her quietly. 'That's why I behaved myself!'

'It's never stopped you before!' She had done it again, she realised when she saw his face, and bit her lip anxiously on further indiscretions. Heaven knew what he was thinking of her for protesting so much about his behaving properly and she looked at him through the concealment of her lashes for a moment. 'I—I suppose I was a bit—happy,' she admitted after a second or two, and Kai smiled, shaking his head.

'Granted!' he agreed quietly. 'Now let's say no more about it, shall we?'

'Kai——'

He leaned across the table and placed one long finger on her lips, so lightly it was almost a caress. 'Quiet!' he said firmly. 'Change the subject, O.K.?'

She nodded, but before she could say anything there were sounds of someone in the hall and after a second or two Calvin appeared, his grey eyes expressing dislike of that intimate breakfast table. 'Good morning,' he said shortly. 'I thought you'd be through with breakfast by now.'

Kate shook her head. 'Not after dancing until nearly three this morning!' she told him with a smile, then realised that last night's affair was hardly the most tactful subject to raise.

He ignored Kai, apart from a brief nod, and came to stand beside Kate, one hand in a suggestively possessive gesture on her shoulder. 'I wondered if you'd like to come swimming,' he said, and Kate nodded eagerly.

'I'd love to,' she said readily enough, and for the first time since his arrival Calvin smiled, his hand on her shoulder pressing firmly into her soft flesh.

'Good, I thought maybe you'd be glad of some fresh air after last night!'

Kate got up, anxious to be away, for she always found it too embarrassing if Kai and Calvin were together for any length of time. Not that they were likely to quarrel, but Calvin never made any secret of his dislike and Kai, instead of giving him the satisfaction of disliking him in return, merely seemed to find his antagonism amusing, which only made things worse.

Kai was looking behind her now and raising a brow, and a hasty glance revealed Mrs. Leith coming in with her breakfast. 'I think you'd better eat first,' he suggested *sotto voce*, 'otherwise Mrs. Leith's going to start kicking up. You're already late, sending your breakfast back isn't going to pour oil on troubled waters!'

'Oh dear!' Kate saw the truth of what he said, despite her readiness to go with Calvin. 'I suppose I'd better eat it.'

'Not if you don't want it,' Calvin interposed swiftly. 'Nobody's going to be unreasonable about it.' He turned to Mrs. Leith and put a hand on her arm, smiling persuasively. 'Kate isn't hungry this morning,' he told her. 'You don't mind, do you, Mother?'

It was the first time he had openly acknowledged the relationship, and Kate noticed how he glanced at her as he did so, with an almost defiant look in his eyes. Mrs. Leith's sharp gaze flicked swiftly from Kate to her son, then she shrugged her narrow shoulders and turned back to the kitchen, still carrying the tray.

'Makes no difference to me,' she declared shortly. 'I guess wasting a little food doesn't matter now and then when there's plenty.'

'Problem solved!' said Calvin, and tucked his arm under Kate's again with that air of possessiveness that somehow troubled her. 'Now let's go, honey, huh?'

Kate nodded, glancing curiously at Kai when he

144

too got to his feet. He leaned over the balcony and pulled a heavy-headed yellow blossom from one of the vines that grew on the balcony, and looking at her steadily for a moment he smiled. Then in one stride he was beside her again and tucking the yellow allamanda flower firmly into her hair behind her left ear.

'Don't forget you're spoken for,' he reminded her in a deep soft voice that turned Calvin's good-looking features a bright indignant pink.

'You've got one hell of a nerve!' he told Kai harshly. 'On the strength of one evening out you figure you have the right to act like you *own* Kate? No chance!' He snatched the offending blossom from her hair and she let out a faint cry when he also pulled some of her hair with it. Then flinging it over the edge of the balcony into the ocean he glared at Kai angrily. 'You just better learn, Fernandez,' he told him in a voice that shook with anger, 'you can't have any woman you want—not when it's Kate, you can't!'

Kai, quite unmoved, if his expression was anything to judge by, perched himself on the rail that ran round the edge of the balcony, balanced above the sea and the rocks below. One foot swinging nonchalantly, he looked at Kate and not at his antagonist. 'Hadn't you better get Kate's opinion on that?' he suggested softly.

Calvin must have felt very sure of his ground, for he did not even look at Kate to ask her opinion, he simply moved across until he stood directly in front of Kai as he maintained his precarious balance on the balcony rail. 'I guess I could solve a whole lot of

145

problems by shoving you over that rail,' he said in a tight cold voice, and Kate shook her head urgently, pushing past the little table to get to him.

'Oh no, Cal, please!' She put a hand on his arm, horribly uncertain how serious his threat was, but knowing that Kai's look of cool contempt must infuriate him further. 'Cal, please!'

'Oh, don't worry,' Calvin told her harshly. 'I don't see him as worth the trouble it would cause.' He looked at Kai with his grey eyes hard and flinty as stone. 'Just don't push where Kate's concerned,' he warned him. 'She's not your exclusive property and she isn't going to be just another of your— your pushovers. O.K.?'

Kai glanced back at Kate again and his wide mouth held a hint of devilment that was echoed in the glittering darkness of his eyes. She knew he was recalling her jibe only a few minutes ago about his being so reticent when he left her last night, and he was teasing her about it without saying a word.

She sometimes wished she didn't have that strange sense of rapport with him, for it was both disturbing and embarrassing, and she hastily avoided his eyes as she tugged at Calvin's arm, while she shook her head in reproach at Kai. 'Let's go, Cal,' she urged quietly. 'There's really no need to make a fuss about anything.'

A confrontation like this was something Calvin had been wanting, she realised ruefully, and he would relinquish it only reluctantly. 'You don't *mind* him making cracks like that about you?' he asked, and Kate bit her lip. 'You don't mind if he puts some damned pagan symbol on you that marks you as his—his property?'

'Oh, Cal, please don't dramatise!' Kate pleaded. 'It's nothing like that at all.'

Kai, she suspected, would take a long time before his temper reached breaking point, but Calvin's persistence was bound to provoke him and she just couldn't face a full scale showdown between them. Especially not when she was the subject of it.

'Do you *know* what he was implying by putting that flower in your hair?' Calvin insisted, and she took his arm firmly and pulled him away, out of Kai's reach.

'It was simply carrying on a joke we started last night,' she told him, making it sound as matter-of-fact as possible. 'Now, please, Cal!'

'But to them it means——'

'I know what it means,' Kate told him hastily. 'I know all about it, but it was said only in fun, Cal. Now please come before I change my mind!'

He went with her, but only reluctantly, and she turned as they reached the doorway and looked back at Kai, outlined like some darkly colourful carving against the bright morning sky and the restless blue of the ocean. He belonged, he was *kamaaina* and he was proud of it.

It spoke volumes about Calvin's attitude, Kate thought as they crossed the hall and went out into the sunlight. 'To them', he had said, meaning Kai and every other native-born Hawaiian. They were a race apart to him and he made no bones about it. Calvin would never be anything other than *mali-hini*, and she wondered if it was simply dislike or sheer envy that made him so bitter.

They drove round to somewhere further along the coast, a spot that Calvin knew and he had said little as they drove there. The sea was bright and clear and much more placid in this small bay where so few people came, and they had been swimming for nearly an hour.

There were no rollers here, so Kate had no fear of being capsized by the surf. Pleasantly tired after their swim, they stretched out on brightly coloured beach wraps in the sun, their bodies still wet from the sea but rapidly drying out in the warm sun.

Calvin seemed to be much less tense now, his earlier anger with Kai apparently forgotten or at least temporarily put to the back of his mind, and Kate thought how much younger he looked as he lay there with his eyes closed and his features relaxed. He was quite incredibly good-looking too and not in the least like Kai.

Kate, propped up on one elbow beside him, looked out at the glinting, ever-shifting surface of the ocean and pushed her sunglasses further up the bridge of her nose. She always enjoyed swimming with Calvin, he was good company and he was also charmingly good-mannered, but somehow this morning she found it much harder to keep Kai completely out of mind.

Last night had been something rather special, that fact kept coming back to her. It was her first really big social event, it was true, but it was difficult not to attribute most of her enjoyment to being in Kai's company, and she realised with an inward sigh that Kai was becoming much too much a part of her life lately. She had to admit it, but she was not at all sure that it was a good thing.

Ever since she had arrived at Hale Makai she seemed to have been involved with him in one way or another. For one thing it was difficult not to take a personal and rather intimate view of someone who shared her breakfast table, then he had snatched her from the surf, half-drowned, and breathed life back into her.

He had been comforting but exciting after she had tried unsuccessfully to emulate his skill underwater and he seemed to be able to coax her out of her anger more successfully than anyone else—he was far too much a part of her life, and she was well aware that he could also cause her a good deal of hurt if she allowed herself to become too attracted to him.

Perhaps Iolani Fernandez and Marjie Van Koren thought of him as part of their lives too, and heaven knew how many others. There was little about Kai that suggested he would ever make the kind of steady and reliable husband that her family wanted for her, and yet in some strange way she felt comforted by him whenever she was in need of reassurance.

She glanced down at her companion and smiled ruefully—Calvin was probably a much safer proposition as a husband, and she already knew he was in love with her and yet somehow she could never see herself married to Calvin. Charming as he was he lacked that special something that Kai had, and he certainly had never played such havoc with her emotions as Kai could.

'Honey?' He smiled up at her enquiringly as if

her preoccupation troubled him, and reached for her hand. 'Are you bored?' he asked, and Kate shook her head hastily, glad of those concealing dark lenses.

'No, of course I'm not bored!' she denied. 'How could anyone be bored with all this *and* a good-looking man for company?'

'Good-looking enough to marry?' Calvin asked quietly.

He sat up suddenly and put an arm round her waist, looking at her with anxious grey eyes, and Kate smiled. She put a hand to his face, gently, almost consolingly, and wished she could say yes as easily as she felt she ought to be able to. But it was impossible when she was so uncertain of her feelings—and then there was Kai—she shrugged impatiently.

'I wish I could,' she told Calvin softly. 'I only wish I could say yes, Cal, but——' She shook her head, unwilling to hurt him but seeing no other way but to be honest. 'You'd be hurt if I said yes and—and didn't mean it.'

He was silent for several minutes, sitting with his legs drawn up and his forearms resting on his knees, in an oddly defensive attitude, and Kate wondered what was going on in his mind as he gazed out at the water. 'You didn't turn a hair when I called—when I spoke to my mother,' he said at last, and Kate's pulses leapt anxiously. 'You knew all along, didn't you, Kate?'

'I knew,' she confirmed quietly, wondering where this new frankness was going to lead. 'I'm only surprised you didn't tell me yourself. Why didn't you, Cal?'

'Because there's more to it than just—what you know already,' Calvin said quietly. He still didn't look at her while he spoke and she could see how taut his knuckles looked although his hands weren't actually clenched. 'I wonder Fernandez hasn't take the opportunity to tell you the whole story,' he added bitterly. 'It wouldn't have surprised me!'

'Kai told me nothing apart from the fact that Mrs. Leith is your mother,' she said. At the back of her mind she suspected he anticipated, almost hoped, she would leap fiercely to Kai's defence, but she refused to be drawn into quarrelling with him about Kai. 'He said that if I wanted to know any more I'd have to ask you,' she told him, and he laughed shortly.

'Big of him!' he jeered, and glowered at the shimmering ocean angrily. 'He shares the same view as the rest of them, of course—that the old man was incapable of doing anything mean and underhand, they all think—— Oh hell!' he said in sudden despair. 'What's the use!'

Kate's heart was rapping urgently at her ribs as she looked at him and she licked her lips before she could speak, because they were suddenly dry. 'If it's something to do with my uncle,' she told him quietly, 'I think you should tell me what it is, Cal. I have the right to know and maybe I could—put it right.'

'I wish to God I knew what rights *I* have!' Calvin declared angrily, then shook his head slowly as if to clear it. 'I'm sorry, Kate, it isn't your doing, but I've lived with this thing all my life and I'm sick of taking the sticky end of something that was none of *my* doing either!'

'Cal——' He put a hand over hers and shook his head.

'There's nothing you can do to change things,' he said in a hard, flat voice, 'but I might as well tell you the whole story, because sooner or later somebody's going to.' He gazed out at the water again, as if he sought the right words to begin. 'You know what the old man was like,' he said at last. 'About women, I mean.' He turned briefly to look at her. 'Or did you?' he asked, and Kate shook her head.

'There were rumours,' she admitted, 'but never anything definite. I don't think anyone heard from him after I was born and no one spoke about him very often, when they did it was usually all innuendo and shaking heads, nothing specific.'

'He liked women,' Calvin declared shortly, 'all the time I knew him, and he was getting on for eighty when I first came here! Years ago he had quite a reputation for being a charmer, he never looked his age, and——' Calvin hesitated and his features were set into a cold look of distaste. Kate, realising how hard it must be for him, put a hand on his arm in sympathy. 'Mother wasn't always the way she is now,' he went on. 'She was quite a good-looking woman and she was as vulnerable as the rest to Charles Wilmot's charm.'

'Mrs. Leith?' It was hard for Kate to see that stern, unyielding figure as the victim of passion, but she was bound to believe him in the circumstances.

'She was Miss Aldyce then,' Calvin said, 'and working for one of the wealthy families in Honolulu, though she came from the mainland originally. Charles Wilmot was a friend of the family and he lost no time noticing how attractive their maid was—and apparently neither did the family chauffeur. As I said Mother was a very attractive woman in those days and she wasn't averse to having two admirers, but when she found she was expecting a child, it was a different story, of course—neither of them wanted to know!'

'Oh, Cal!'

For the first time, Kate found it possible to allow for that permanently sour expression of Mrs. Leith's and she felt an impulsive and genuine pity for her, despite her apparent promiscuity.

'The old man was in his late fifties then, of course,' Calvin went on, apparently determined to see it to the bitter end, 'so it wasn't impossible that the child was his, although he denied it and went on denying it. The family she worked for more or less forced their chauffeur to marry her, but the day after the wedding he disappeared back to the mainland and she never saw him again. Mother had me in the Honolulu hospital, but she never knew who paid the hospital bills—certainly it wasn't her missing husband—then she sent me across to the mainland to my grandmother. It wasn't difficult for her to get a divorce, and she stayed on here to work.'

He sat for a moment saying nothing, and Kate was loath to speak in case he took it for mere curiosity. 'The old man never married,' he went on, after a moment, 'and I think it was that decided Mother to fix on him as my father. He was unmarried and already pretty wealthy, and she felt she had a claim on him, but he never would marry her, and eventually, after sixteen years, she married Andy Leith, a clerk at the bank.'

'Poor woman!' Kate said softly. 'I never realised, Cal, just what she's been through.'

'I guess most folks don't care,' Cal said flatly. 'They just figure that any trouble she got she brought on herself.' He shrugged, his mouth bitter. 'Who knows?' he asked harshly. 'Maybe they're right!'

'Oh but, Cal, you can't blame any one person in a case like that,' Kate objected. 'How can you? Maybe Uncle Charles wasn't—maybe he wasn't your father, but if it was possible he was then he should have owned up!'

'And if he wasn't?' Calvin asked bitterly. 'Why should he have done?' He was silent again for a while, looking at the sea and holding his hands tightly together. 'She was quite settled with Andy Leith I think, for a while, then he was ill and finally he died, so she was on her own again. To give him his due old Charlie did take pity on her then, he took her in as his housekeeper, and when I came over he gave me the job as his secretary—it was the nearest he ever came to acknowledging me as his son and I think Mother took hope from it. That will of his was the biggest blow she ever had, I think.'

Kate took a moment to consider who was really to blame in the whole sorry mess. She could hardly claim to be surprised that Mrs. Leith named Charles Wilmot as the possible father of her child, for she herself had wondered whether Kai was his son. But the fact of the other man as well made it much less easy to put blame on anyone except the same person who had borne it for most of the past twenty-six years or so, and once again she pitied Mrs. Leith in her bitterness.

'Was—do you really think Uncle Charles *was* your father, Cal?' she asked eventually, and he shook his head, a frown of impatience drawing at his brows.

'How do I know?' he asked harshly. 'How *could* I know, Kate? I simply know what Mother's told me, and that she expected him to leave the bulk of his money to me, as a—a kind of last gesture! I don't even know if she really believes it herself, or if she's just talked herself into it over the years. She believed we should have had that money—that he owed it to her for what happened.'

'And you?' Kate prompted gently, and Calvin shook his head, running his fingers through his hair in a gesture of despair.

'I just don't know, Kate, I just don't know!'

'No one else believed it?' she asked, and he shrugged.

'Everyone liked the old man, I did myself, he was very easy to like,' Calvin said, 'and I did expect to inherit more than I did when he died, but——' He shrugged his shoulders again with such an air of resignation that Kate felt a surge of almost unbearable pity for him in his dilemma. 'I guess it was his way of having the last word,' he said flatly. 'Maybe his friends are right—he wouldn't have snubbed me so definitely if he thought I *was* his son.'

They were both silent for several minutes, watching the sea roll lazily in and out, and the bright glitter of the sun on the waves. It was so quiet and peaceful that it was difficult to imagine that such turmoil could exist as made Calvin so angry and uncertain.

Kate, in her own heart, felt convinced that if Charles Wilmot had been Calvin's father, or had any idea that he could be, he would have made some admission of it, even if it was only at the last, by leaving him his rightful inheritance. The fact that he had not done so was, to Kate at least, a pretty certain indication that Mrs. Leith had lied and, much as she pitied Calvin as the innocent pawn in the game, she could not bring herself to blame her great-uncle.

'Kate?' Calvin turned towards her again and took her hands in his, his grey eyes searching her face for some clue to what she was thinking, his fingers tensing tightly around hers. 'This'll make a difference, won't it?' he asked, and Kate looked at him uncomprehendingly for a moment. 'About your feelings for me, I mean,' he said.

Kate shook her head urgently. 'Oh no, Cal, of course it won't!' How could she let it make a difference? she thought wildly. If she did he was bound to take it far harder than any other man would after a refusal to marry him. 'You're still the same person,' she told him, anxious to reassure him. 'No matter who your father was I still feel— well, that you're someone special, Cal.'

His eyes held hers for a moment, blank with disbelief, then he smiled. 'Someone—special?' he asked softly, and Kate nodded, uncertain now, that she had said the right thing. 'Oh, Kate!' There was no mistaking the sudden look of pleasure that lit up his face, and for a moment Kate felt a cold rush of panic and her stomach curled at the realisation of what she might have said.

'Cal, if you——' She tried to stop it, but it was too late now.

'You *will* marry me!' He cut her explanation short and leaned forward to press his mouth to hers with a fierceness that was less a caress than a gesture of relief, she thought. 'Oh, Kate, darling Kate, you've made me so *happy!*'

'But please, Cal——' Again she tried to stop him, to explain, but it was no use. In her pity she had allowed herself to give a wrong impression and it would take a callousness she was incapable of to reject him now.

'I can't believe it!' Calvin whispered against her tumbled hair. 'I just can't believe it, darling!' He raised his head for a brief second and laughed. '*Now* let Fernandez get any big ideas about you, or about staying in the beach house! I'll take him apart if he as much as lays a finger on you—and we'll have him out of that beach house so fast he'll never know what happened to him!'

Kai! Kate stiffened suddenly in his arms and her eyes, as they gazed across Calvin's shoulder, were wide and blank with dismay. Of course Kai would be one of the first to know, and she didn't know how she could face him and tell him that she had been foolish enough to give Calvin the wrong impression about her feelings, simply by being too sympathetic.

He would know how it had happened, inevitably, and if she knew Kai, he would make it his business to do something about it. She had to admit as she sat there with Calvin, that she prayed Kai *would* do something about it, for she saw little hope of helping herself.

CHAPTER NINE

IT was later the same day, when Kate came in to dinner, that she heard raised voices coming from the direction of the kitchen and she frowned uneasily. One of the voices belonged unmistakably to Kai, although heaven knew what he was doing in the kitchen. While she still hesitated, standing half way between the stairs and the dining-room, he came hurrying out of the kitchen into the hall, his dark eyes still gleaming with the light of battle.

Seeing Kate, he came to a sudden halt and for a moment she thought he was about to attack her too, for there was a dark glittering look in his eyes that betrayed more anger than she had ever seen there before. Then he laughed shortly and ran one hand through the thick blackness of his hair, shaking his head slowly.

'I'm eating out,' he told her, as if she expected an explanation. 'But you'll be O.K. for a dinner at least!'

'I'll be——' she began, and blinked at him uncomprehendingly for a moment.

Kai clucked his tongue impatiently. 'It's the end of the month,' he reminded her, 'I guess you forgot, huh? Mrs. Leith packed her bags,' he went on with obvious restraint. 'It looks like we'll go hungry tomorrow morning!'

Kate put a hand to her mouth, her eyes wide and understanding at last. 'Oh, Kai, I'd forgotten!'

It seemed barely credible that a whole month had passed since Mrs. Leith had met her in the hall one morning and informed her that she would be leaving Hale Makai at the end of the month. Kate supposed she should have done something about it, obviously Kai thought she should have done, but somehow the time had sped by all too swiftly and she had done nothing.

'So I gathered!' Kai remarked dryly, and his tone was enough to arouse her resentment. After all, his welfare was as much concerned as her own.

'I don't see why I have——' she began, but he waved her to silence with a large hand, and shook his head impatiently.

'I don't have time to listen to explanations,' he informed her with unusal brusqueness. 'I'm going out!'

'I don't *have* to explain!' Kate called out after him as he went across the hall with long impatient strides, and he turned in the doorway, looking across at her with dark, unfathomable eyes.

'You've got a whole lot of explaining to do, honey,' he told her, and waved a hand in that careless half salute she was beginning to recognise. '*Aloha*, Kate!'

Kate didn't bother to reply, she made her way to the dining-room and sat down to her solitary dinner. His last words had disturbed her and somehow she felt that everything at Hale Makai was about to change, that nothing would ever be the same again, and it gave her a curious sense of sadness.

The following morning when Kate came downstairs she found not only Kai waiting for her in the hall, but a round-faced, plump Hawaiian woman, and she frowned at them curiously. The woman was middle-aged, her dark hair going grey, and there was a network of fine wrinkles all over her brown face, but she looked friendly and Kate smiled instinctively when she said good morning.

'Good morning, Kate!' Kai beamed her a smile, so obviously his temper of last night was over. 'This is Luana,' he said, urging the woman forward with him. 'Our temporary new housekeeper; Luana, this is Miss Wilmot.'

'*Aloha*, Miss Wilmot!' The woman smiled, a broad and friendly Hawaiian smile, and Kate could do no other than respond. This large cheerful woman in her colourful and voluminous *muumuu* was a distinct improvement on Mrs. Leith, but her being there puzzled her for the moment.

'*Aloha*, Luana!' She returned the greeting readily enough, then looked at Kai curiously. 'Our housekeeper?' she said. 'Have you——'

'I thought somebody ought to do something about it,' Kai told her coolly. 'Mrs. Leith's evidently decided to give us breakfast before she leaves, after all, but I guessed you wouldn't have done anything about replacing her, so I got Luana to stand in for a while until you can get somebody to suit you.'

'Well, I've scarcely had time since last night,' Kate retorted, and Kai shook his head.

'You've had a whole month,' he reminded her.

Stung to her own defence, Kate looked at him down the length of her small nose. 'I don't remem-

161

ber there being any hard and fast rule that *I* had to be the one to hire the staff,' she told him. 'Hale Makai is as much yours as it is mine and you've as much at stake as I have if we're left to fend for ourselves!'

It sounded rather disturbingly intimate somehow, to be talking like that, and she was glad that Calvin wasn't there to hear her, or he would surely have raised some objection. Kai, of course, seemed to be treating the whole thing as a joke, and his dark eyes glistened with laughter as he looked at her.

'I'd fare all right,' he told her with a grin. 'I don't know what your qualifications are as a cook!'

'I can cook,' Kate informed him haughtily. 'I'm also capable of keeping house, English style, but it probably wouldn't suit you. Anyway,' she added as an afterthought, 'I don't see why I should keep house when I've just inherited all that money!'

'Ha ha!' He glanced at Luana, who seemed to wear a permanent broad smile on her brown face and was apparently enjoying the exchange enormously. 'Heiresses don't do such menial tasks, is *that* what you're telling me? Well, since it's beneath your dignity to take on a new housekeeper as well, it's just as well I got Luana to come!'

He was being deliberately provocative, that was certain, and Kate knew she should have known better than to allow herself to be so provoked, but somehow with Kai the temptation was always there and irresistible.

'You seem to have done very well,' she told him. 'Can't we keep Luana full time?'

'Unfortunately not,' Kai told her, and glanced down at the woman, winking broadly, a gesture that sent her into a loud fit of giggles. 'She has a brood of her own to look after and it wasn't easy persuading her, but I managed it eventually!'

'Of course!' Kate ignored his soft tut-tut of reproach and gave her attention to their temporary housekeeper. 'I'm very grateful to you, Luana,' she told her. 'I hope it won't be too much of a nuisance to you and your family, coming here.'

'No nuisance!' Luana assured her cheerfully. 'My fella don' mine if I come some time—not all time!'

Kate really felt rather helpless about finding anyone else and she looked at Kai again, wishing he would be a little more co-operative. He must surely know where it was possible to get someone to keep house for them and yet he was making little attempt to offer advice.

His eyes were watching her, glittering with amusement or, she could scarcely believe, malice, and she felt strangely disturbed by them somehow. She found the dark, unfathomable gaze unnerving, for it was almost as if he enjoyed her discomfiture, and that hurt more than she cared to admit.

'Kai,' she said at last in a small uncertain voice, 'could you—I mean, I don't know anything about taking on——'

'Maybe you should get Cal to help you,' he suggested, and Kate flushed. She looked uneasily at Luana and wondered what on earth she was making of this somewhat garbled and very personal exchange.

For some reason he had seen fit to bring Calvin into it, and Kate wondered why. Calvin was another problem she had yet to find a solution to before too long, but Kai was unlikely to be much help there either in his present mood. He seemed to be deliberately trying to make things difficult for her and it made her angry as well as hurt.

'You seem to be pretty good at persuading wives to leave their husbands,' she told him shortly, 'maybe you could find one who'll make it permanent!'

Luana seemed to follow the suggestion easily enough despite the fact that it was not in her more familiar pidgin, and she laughed uproariously, nudging Kai in the ribs and rocking back and forth on her heels. 'Your *wahine* know you good, *kanaka!*' she told him, and Kai flicked a dark brow swiftly upwards.

'My *wahine* says too damned much!' he said softly, and Luana laughed loudly, her dark eyes twinkling with mischief, while Kate turned hastily and went into the breakfast room. She knew well enough that *wahine* meant woman, but she simply hadn't the nerve to stand there and try to explain to Luana that she wasn't Kai's woman—she would never have believed her anyway.

They had finished their breakfast, provided rather grudgingly by Mrs. Leith, and Kate now wondered how she had come to say so much to Kai about the situation she was in with Calvin. She hadn't intended to tell him, not after his behaviour over the housekeeper, but somehow Kai could persuade anything from anyone if he put his mind to it.

It seemed to Kate almost as if he had known already, and yet she didn't see how it was possible. She had said little while they ate, but gradually, under Kai's skilful prompting she had told him all of it. It was his questions that had, in fact, made her suspect that he had prior knowledge.

It was difficult to meet his eyes, but Kai was determined that she should, and she hastily looked away again whenever she felt herself about to succumb. She still sat at the little table on the balcony, with the remains of their breakfast still uncleared, and tried to look composed. In reality her heart was hammering so hard at her ribs that it was making her breathless and she found herself with an inexplicable tingle of excitement stirring her pulses.

Kai, perched on the balcony rail but near enough to be disturbing, looked down at her for several seconds as if she had taken leave of her senses. Then he slid one large hand under her chin and lifted her face to him, shaking his head as if in despair. 'You're a crazy little idiot,' he said quietly, and briefly his strong fingers gripped her jaw hard. 'How could you be so *dumb*, you little dope?'

'Stop calling me names and look at it from my point of view,' Kate told him shortly, turning her face away. 'I wish I hadn't told you now, I might have known you'd be too insensitive to understand!'

'You're wrong on all counts, as usual,' Kai told her without malice. 'For one thing *you* didn't tell me, you only confirmed what I already knew.'

Kate blinked at him, her suspicions confirmed. 'You knew?' she asked, and he nodded.

'Cal was here at the crack of dawn to break the good news to me, he just had to crow! What's more,' he went on relentlessly, 'Mrs. Leith told me about it even earlier—last night, to be exact.'

'Oh!' Once again Kate hastily avoided his eyes and her heart was thudding almost painfully hard at her ribs. 'So that's why——'

'Why I ate out last night,' he finished for her. 'If I'd stayed and shared your dinner I'd probably have strangled you in sheer desperation!'

It was just exaggerated enough to be true, Kate recognised, and chanced an upward glance. 'I don't know how it happened,' she said. 'I felt—I don't know exactly.'

'I understand exactly how you felt,' Kai informed her. 'You see, I'm not as insensitive as you seem to think! You felt sorry for him because he told you about that business between his mother and Charlie, isn't that so?'

'Couldn't it be true?' Kate challenged, and Kai shook his head slowly.

'God knows,' he said quietly, 'but whether it is or not makes no difference to your problem!'

'It makes me not want to hurt him any more,' Kate declared firmly. 'He's had to put up with a lot because of what happened all those years ago, Kai, you wouldn't understand how he feels.'

'Would you?' Kai countered swiftly, and she looked down again at her hands, her mouth showing a hint of reproach in a slight pout.

'Maybe not from personal experience,' she allowed reluctantly. 'But I do feel sorry for him, for all he's had to suffer over the years, and it makes it worse that Uncle Charles was partly responsible for what happened.'

'You don't know that,' Kai argued quietly, and Kate looked at him uncertainly.

Kai had known her uncle perhaps better than anyone and it might be possible that in an unguarded moment he had confided in him. 'Do you know he wasn't?' she asked quietly. 'It's an admitted fact that Uncle Charles—liked women, and——'

'So do I,' Kai interrupted impatiently, 'but I don't expect to be called upon to pay for it for the rest of my life!'

'But Cal——'

'Knows only as much as his mother's told him,' Kai insisted firmly. 'There's no proof that Charlie Wilmot was his father, Kate, no proof at all, only the bitter ravings of a woman who considers she got the worst of a bargain. Old Charlie paid for over twenty-five years for casting his roving eye on the Calworths' pretty maid—you've got no call to add your five cents' worth, Kate, so don't act so self-righteous about it!'

'Kai!' She looked at him reproachfully and, after a second or two he smiled ruefully and shook his head. 'Anyway,' she went on, 'I feel sorry for Cal, no matter who was to blame.'

Kai sighed despairingly, then raised her chin again, lifting her face to him and bending over her until his breath warmed her mouth while he spoke. 'But, honey,' he explained patiently, 'you didn't have to promise to marry the guy to show him how sorry you are.'

'I didn't promise,' Kate objected, 'that's the trouble, I wouldn't mind if I had or even if I wanted to——' She stopped short there and shook her head.

'Which you don't?' Kai suggested, and she hastily bit her lip. 'Then you should have corrected that wrong impression right there and then, honey. You're going to have one hell of a job getting out of this now, you realise that, don't you?'

Kate shrugged helplessly. An attempt to evade his hand on her chin resulted in his capturing her hand instead, and he now held both of them in his, his long thumbs moving caressingly over her palms. Perched as he was on the balcony rail beside her, he was much too close for comfort, and Kate wished he would move somewhere else, and then perhaps she could think more clearly.

'Maybe I shouldn't *try* to get out of it,' she began, and gasped aloud when he snatched at her hands and pulled her to her feet.

Pressing her palms flat against the warmth of his body, he held her firmly with his eyes only inches from hers, trying again to hold her gaze. Her hands were trembling and she felt quite dizzy with the pounding of the pulse at her temple. 'You know damned well you want to get out of it,' he told her. 'Don't try and deny it, Kate—I shan't believe you!'

'Believe what you like!' Kate felt suddenly and unexpectedly lightheaded, and she tried hard to control her voice and the trembling in her hands.

'Kate!' He spoke softly, and she felt a shiver slide along her spine like an icy finger.

She tried again to snatch her hands away, but he held her too tightly, looking down at her with glittering eyes, his strong fingers squeezed hers briefly as if to remind her that she hadn't a hope of escaping until he allowed her to do so. 'I'm not so sure it would be so bad being married to Cal,' she told him breathlessly. 'He—he's good-looking and—and at least I'd know where I was with him! I'd know there wouldn't be any—any Marjie Van Korens hiding behind bushes with him!'

'Why, you little——' He gripped her tightly again and her heart beat so wildly in panic that she almost choked. Then suddenly he laughed, shaking his head, his eyes glittering darkly at her. 'You can't forget that, can you?' he asked, and held her hands against the smooth dark gold of his chest. 'Did it bother you so much, Kate, to find me kissing Marjie Van Koren—or Iolani, maybe?' She refused to answer but tried again to free her hands, but he held them tight and shook her lightly. 'Kate?'

'It didn't bother me at all!' she denied breathlessly. 'I know what you're like—you can't shock me, and I really don't *care* what you do with Marjie Van Koren, or anyone else!'

'No?' he laughed again, and Kate's green eyes blazed at him angrily.

'No!' she declared, shaking her head and trying hard to sound as if she meant it.

Whenever she thought about him with Marjie Van Koren or anyone else she found herself caring more all the time and it disturbed her. Calvin couldn't play such havoc with her emotions as Kai could and she wished with all her heart that he did, it would make things so much easier for her in the end.

'For your information,' she told him in a voice that would shake despite her efforts to steady it, 'I shan't do anything about Cal at all. I'll just let things go on as they are—I'll marry him, as he wants me to!'

'*Oh* no, Kate!' He held her hands tight against him, his eyes glittering as he shook his head firmly. 'You can't *do* that, it wouldn't be fair to the poor guy. Don't use him to get at me—you don't play that dirty, honey!'

'To get at——' She looked at him with bright, shining green eyes and drew a deep breath when her pulses quickened at the look that fastened itself immovably on her mouth. 'Give me one good reason why I can't marry him!' she challenged huskily, and Kai was shaking his head again, a hint of that crooked smile twitching at his wide mouth.

He looked at her steadily for a moment while her heart beat so wildly in her breast that she felt it would stop, then his hands released hers suddenly and went instead to the small of her back. Pressed towards him until she stood within touching distance of that steely, masculine warmth, she shivered.

One hand took her firmly by the back of her head and the other swept her against him while his mouth bore down on hers with a fierceness that took her breath away. It was a hard and determined assault on her senses, forcing her lips apart, as ruthless as it was exciting, and briefly she fought against it as she had done before.

Soon, however, the first wild panic left her and she yielded instead to the unfamiliar fierceness of her own desires. Sliding her arms up around his neck, she twined her fingers in the thick blackness of his hair, responding with every nerve in her body to the urgent claims he made on her, her eyes closed as she pressed even closer to the vigorous masculine force that made demands she had never experienced before.

It was a long time before she was aware of anyone else in the room, and then a certain chill certainty of being watched touched some nerve in her subconscious and sent a little shiver along her spine in warning.

Breathless and shaking like a leaf, she turned swiftly in time to see Mrs. Leith just leaving the room, soft-footed and unobtrusive, her straight back making its own comment. Kate watched her go, still tight in the circle of Kai's arms, too stunned for a moment to do anything other than stare.

Then she pushed at the hands that still held her and stepped back hastily, her eyes wide and uncertain. 'She'll tell Cal,' she whispered, and Kai frowned.

'Sure she'll tell Cal,' he agreed, a hint of impatience in his voice. 'Maybe that's the answer, Kate!'

'Oh no!' Kate looked at him with reproachful eyes, shaking her head. If she was to break with Calvin it must be in her own way, by explaining as kindly as she could how the mistake had occurred, not through his mother telling how she had seen her with Kai. 'I couldn't let him find out that way,' she told him. 'I couldn't, Kai.'

'Then how?' he asked quietly, sitting back on the balcony rail again, and Kate shook her head.

She looked at him, her eyes appealing. Surely he couldn't refuse to help her, to give her some idea what she should do about Calvin. He had ended affairs, he would know how to say the right things that didn't hurt too much. 'Help me, Kai,' she whispered. 'I don't want to hurt him.'

For a moment he said nothing, but his eyes, dark and unfathomable as ever, lingered on her mouth as if it fascinated him. Then he got up, toweringly tall against the bright blue morning sky, shaking his head slowly. 'Somebody's going to get hurt, Kate,' he said quietly. 'Who it is I guess is up to you.' He made no explanation of his words, but simply bent and brushed his mouth lightly across hers. '*Aloha*, honey.'

Someone had to be hurt, Kai had said, and as far as Kate could see it was almost bound to be Calvin. For a long time she had sat in the shade of the palm trees that straggled almost to the ocean's edge, and now she sat on the balcony that ran by her bedroom, but still the questions remained unanswered.

Impatient with her inability to deal with her own problems, she got to her feet and leaned on the balcony rail, looking out at the shimmering expanse of the sea and wishing she had the peace of mind to enjoy what should have been a paradise. It was no use brooding about Calvin, as Kai had said, the only way was to be honest with him and let him know as soon as possible that she couldn't marry him.

She sighed, facing the task unwillingly, then held her breath when the sound of voices came from the room below, carried clearly on the still air and easily identifiable. Calvin was visiting his mother and their conversation was going to be perfectly audible to her if she stayed where she was.

Hating the thought of eavesdropping, she was about to turn away when she caught the sound of her own name and paused. Calvin's voice was asking where she was, then Mrs. Leith's flat, sharp tones telling him, 'She went down to the beach earlier, I guess she's still there.'

Expecting that Calvin would go looking for her, Kate leaned over the balcony to call to him, but once again he spoke and she hesitated, her heart thudding in her breast as she fought to still her conscience. 'If she's with Fernandez I'll hit him!' he declared harshly, and Kate bit her lip hard at the tone he used. Never had she heard him so bitter and angry, and he sounded capable of doing what he said.

'You'd better marry her as soon as possible,' Mrs. Leith's sharp voice advised him bluntly. 'You nearly let the chance slip once before and he's getting much too friendly for my liking. If you let the whole thing fall through because you've taken too long to talk her round——'

'Mother!' Calvin's cry of protest sounded loud and clear, but Kate was shaking her head slowly back and forth in disbelief, her eyes wide and blank.

'Oh, I know you fell into your own trap,' Mrs. Leith told her son impatiently. 'But you could have married her without falling in love with her!'

'I could have, but I don't have to, as it happens, Mother.' Calvin's quiet insistence did something to ease the awful blankness in Kate's brain and she shook her head, trying to think clearly, while Calvin's voice in the room below still protested his love for her. 'I want to marry her because I love her, not simply because of the money, you know that.'

'Then you get a bonus,' Mrs. Leith allowed shortly. 'You had a right to that money and so did I, and we're going to get it! I've worked all my life for other people, but not any more! I'm through taking orders!'

A brief silence suggested that one or the other was taking a moment for thought, then Calvin's quiet and not very happy voice reached her again. 'Mother, are you sure——' he began, and Kate could easily imagine the look on that good-looking face as he sought for words. 'I mean, no one, no one at all, believes it was old Charlie Wilmot, but you——'

'It doesn't matter one way or the other after all this time,' Mrs. Leith interrupted him shortly, and Calvin's argument was bitter and unexpected.

'It does to me!' he insisted. 'I want to know, Mother!'

Another cold, uneasy silence followed and Kate sat still as a statue on the edge of her bed, shivering despite the warm sunshine that filled her room, her hands clasping the tops of her arms as if to keep warm, her eyes bright with unshed tears. It mattered to her, as well as to Calvin, and she waited for the housekeeper's answer with her eyes tight shut.

'He wanted me,' Mrs. Leith said. 'It amounts to the same!' It was clear that anger burned in her as fiercely as it ever had, despite the passing years. 'He could have married me, but instead he let them marry me off to Hal Morton because I didn't match up to his precious girl-friend in England! He deserved to be made to pay for snubbing me that way, and I mean him to, through that girl! Calvin!' She sounded anxious suddenly, and Kate held her breath, too shaken to move now even if her legs had found the strength to support her. 'You won't back down now, will you?' Mrs. Leith urged her son. 'You want the girl, but you want the money as well, don't you?'

'Yes, yes, of course.' He sounded flat-voiced, resigned, and for a moment Kate could almost find it in her heart to pity him again.

But the whole thing had been carefully planned, that much was clear now. Calvin had approached her in the first place because he wanted her uncle's inheritance—he thought it should have been his, and marrying her was the one way to get it once the will was read.

The thought of his having been so determinedly cold-blooded about it made Kate feel quite sick and she put a hand to her mouth, her eyes closed tight against the prospect of facing him again after learning what kind of a man he was. Kai, she remembered somewhat dazedly, had made a joke about her being a good catch for someone like Calvin—or perhaps he hadn't been joking!

She heard a door close downstairs and somewhere in her numb brain registered that it must be Calvin gone to look for her on the beach. She got to her feet, her breathing short and erratic, and slowly, as she stood there looking out of the window at the bright golden day outside, anger began to replace the stunned daze she had been in.

There was no need to try and break it kindly to Calvin now that she couldn't marry him. It might even serve to ease her wounded pride if she hurt him in return. She picked up her hairbrush and pulled it through the thick brown hair that surrounded her flushed face. She would go and find Calvin, and in no uncertain terms she'd tell him that not only had he lost the money her uncle left, but her too.

The hall was empty and silent when she got downstairs and her footsteps clicked across the floor, short, hasty steps that betrayed her anger. But as she reached the door Mrs. Leith came from the back of the house with her suitcases, and she stared at Kate for a full minute, her hard grey eyes stunned with surprise.

Kate turned and faced her, anger lending her courage even though her hands were shaking and her knees felt dismayingly weak. 'I'm glad you're going, Mrs. Leith,' she told her in a small but quite steady voice. 'I've never had to dismiss anyone and I'd hate to have to start now!'

She did not wait to hear her answer, or even if there was an answer, instead she walked out of the front door and banged it shut behind her. Now if she could only be as bold and determined with Calvin, the whole sordid business would be over.

She found him down under the palm trees, looking rather lost because she wasn't there, and as soon as she saw him she felt her senses rebel against being as harsh with him as she had vowed to be. He turned as she approached and smiled; not his usual smile but a rather tight and uneasy one.

'Kate!' he said softly as she came up to him. 'I've been looking for you!'

She carefully evaded him when he reached out for her, and did not miss the slight frown that drew his brows together. Remaining a foot or so away from him, she tried to put on a bold face, but found it much more difficult than she would have believed.

'Please don't—don't say anything else, Cal,' she told him in a quiet and rather shaky voice. 'I know, you see, I know all about it!'

'Kate?' He was looking at her, only half convinced she wasn't joking.

It was no use keeping him in suspense, nor herself either, and she looked at him, half ashamed of her eavesdropping, even now. 'I—I was in my room when you were talking to your mother, Cal,' she told him quietly, and thanked heaven that she sounded so cool and calm. 'I couldn't help hearing you, but I wish—I almost wish I hadn't. I know now why you wanted to marry me.'

'I love you, Kate!' There was despair in his voice, but he made no attempt to deny it and for that she thanked heaven. At least he was going to be honest about it.

She stood in front of him, the trees casting dark shadows on her face, her lashes hiding the hurt in her eyes. 'I honestly think you do,' she said softly. 'Because I heard you say so to your mother, and you had no reason to lie to her, did you?'

'Kate!' He would have reached for her hands, but she stepped back hastily, and shook her head.

'No, Cal, please don't. It's finished, over, there's no more to be said!'

He stood there for a long moment and she could see that he was trying to find some sort of opening, some extenuating reason, but found none. He shook his head slowly and looked at her at last, his grey eyes dark with a kind of defensive appeal.

'There's nothing I *can* say, is there?' he asked, and she shook her head.

'Goodbye, Cal!'

She turned on her heel and walked back along the beach, quite unconsciously heading past the steps and turning the corner where the beach house sat snug and peaceful among its blossom trees. She heard Calvin, a few seconds later, go hurrying up the wooden steps to the house, and did not even turn her head. There was nothing more to be said.

CHAPTER TEN

THE beach house was deserted when Kate arrived there and she felt oddly let down at not finding Kai. She was in rather a curious mood after the last traumatic half-hour or so and she needed Kai's reassurance more than ever she had. Not quite tearful, but still smarting from the realisation that she had been used to further Mrs. Leith's ambitions, she automatically sought out Kai as a source of comfort.

It did not even strike her as strange that she should turn to Kai when she was in doubt or in need of reassurance, for it seemed like a natural thing to do. Now that it was all over it was easy to realise that she could face the prospect of perhaps not seeing Calvin again, but the thought of a future without Kai was not even bearable.

She sat on a low stone wall surrounding a raised garden that spilled over with every conceivable bloom imaginable, hugging her knees and gazing at the deserted beach house with pensive eyes. She had felt a premonition earlier that morning that everything was about to change and now it had proved right. Nothing at Hale Makai would ever be the same again, and yet she wasn't nearly as regretful as she would have expected.

'Kate?'

She looked up swiftly when Kai's voice brought her out of her reverie. His dark eyes swept over her, curious and speculative and perhaps a little anxious, and he strode across the path to stand beside her. He was paint-stained and untidy and she smiled when she saw him, then, catching his eye, she laughed, because he did and without knowing why she did it, except that she suddenly experienced an unbelievable sense of relief.

'Are you visiting?' Kai asked, and she glanced up at him for a second nodding her head.

'Why not?' she said.

He took both her hands and pulled her from her perch on the wall, one arm sliding easily round her slender waist as he walked with her into the beach house. The familiar warm touch of him tingled through her like wine and she tried hard to steady the frantic beat of her heart. He said nothing for the moment but walked straight across to a small bar in one corner of the big, bright room.

There was nothing English about the beach house, it was purely Hawaiian, built and furnished for eternal summer and with a whole collection of Hawaiian art on shelves round the walls. 'Nice!' Kate remarked, leaving him by the bar and walking across the room to admire some of the pieces. She felt strangely lightheaded, almost as if she was slightly drunk, and every nerve tingled with anticipation.

Kai, over by the bar, poured himself a drink and smiled when she caught his eye briefly. 'Drink?' he asked, and Kate shook her head. He leaned back against the bow-fronted bar and watched her for a moment or two, his eyes dark and unfathomable.

'O.K., honey,' he said quietly at last, 'what happened?'

She picked up a small and rather ugly representation of the goddess Pele and turned it over in her hands rather than look at him. 'I've seen Cal, and it's all finished,' she told him quietly and without drama. 'It was so much easier than I thought it would be.'

Kai took another sip of his drink, still watching her with that steady and rather unnerving gaze. 'Tell me, Kate,' he said, 'what did you do to him?'

Feeling herself under attack, Kate swung round and looked at him with bright, glistening green eyes, her cheeks flushed, angry as always when she was on the defensive. 'What did *I* do?' she asked in a strangely husky voice. 'Do you know what they—Cal and his mother were doing to me?'

Kai took another long drink from his glass then put it down carefully on the bar behind him, turning to face her again slowly. 'They had the money in mind, of course,' he said quietly, and in no doubt that he was right. 'Didn't I warn you about that, honey?'

'You did!' Kate agreed bitterly, and for a second felt that angry prickle of tears again as she looked at him. 'I—I just didn't expect it to hurt so much,' she added with a look in her eyes that showed the hurt.

Kai said nothing for the moment, but he spread his arms wide and she hesitated no more than a second before she went across to him, laying her head on his chest, his arms folded tightly around her, listening to the strong, steady beat of his heart.

'Poor little Kate!' he murmured against her hair.

It was every bit as reassuring as she expected it to be, held in Kai's arms, his face resting on the soft tumble of her hair, and somehow it didn't seem to matter at all about Calvin now. A light, warm kiss on her forehead was followed by a hug that almost crushed the breath from her, and she looked up at him for a second, her eyes searching for something she was not even sure if she'd recognise when she saw it.

'Now that you're here,' he said, as if there was nothing serious in hand at all, 'you can do something for me, will you?'

Kate, curious, if a little disappointed, looked up at him and frowned questioningly. 'What can I possibly do for you?' she asked, and was more puzzled than ever when he laughed softly.

'For starters,' he told her lightly, 'you can help me choose which paintings to send to the Downtown Gallery.'

Kate blinked at him for a moment, her heart fluttering hopefully. To be involved in his work was surely a step in the right direction, and she felt sure he was quite serious about it. 'An exhibition?' she asked, and Kai nodded. 'Oh, Kai, that's marvellous—is it your first?'

He laughed again and shook his head, tolerant of her enthusiasm. 'Heavens, no, honey,' he said softly, 'but I'm naturally pleased about it. It means I can show the people who think I should do only formal portraits that I'm better at something else.'

'And I can help decide which ones to send?' she

asked, full of the idea, and he nodded.

'If you'd like to.' He had no need to ask if she would like to, and he smiled as he led her into another room, probably it had once been another bedroom but it was now a studio, scattered with the usual clutter of an artist. A big, bright sunny room with a breathtaking view of the gardens and the sea.

It was untidy, as she expected, but what paintings she could see stacked around the walls were enough to convince her that the portrait of Charles Wilmot that hung on the staircase at Hale Makai was no fluke. He was a first-class artist and the sight of so much talent affected her strangely, it was almost as if she took a personal pride in it, and she looked around her with an excitement that brought a flush to her cheeks.

There were no formal portraits, but colourful and delightful scenes of island life. Bar-room characters in bright, flowery shirts, girls with their black hair bound with the coronets of melia and ginger blossoms she had seen so often, and landscapes that clearly showed Kai's love of his native islands. At last she knew now what happened on those frequent trips to town with her uncle.

Charles Wilmot liked to sit and watch the kaleidoscope of life going on around him and Kai saw scope for his talent in the dim-lit bars and cafés. It was an odd partnership, but one that must have brought a great deal of pleasure and satisfaction to both men in their respective ways.

'They're all wonderful,' Kate said softly as she looked at one after the other. 'How could anyone choose from so many wonderful things?'

'I have to,' Kai told her with a smile. 'About twenty of them—you bring a fresh eye to them, honey, you help me, huh?'

Only too willing to please, Kate nodded, picking up a small oblong canvas showing a corner of the beach house garden with a magnificent rainbow shower tree in full bloom, its clusters of fluffy heads running from deep pink to pale yellow, so beautiful it looked unreal.

'And this,' she said, handing him another.

It showed Iolani Fernandez curled up on the wall outside the beach house, small and doll-like in an up-to-date version of the voluminous Hawaiian *muumuu*. Kai had captured her expression exactly —teasing, adoring and completely Hawaiian, just as Kate had seen her.

'Iolani?' Kai asked softly, taking it from her, and Kate nodded, refusing to be drawn into discussing Iolani except as the very lovely subject of his painting.

'She's lovely,' she told him, 'and you've captured her so perfectly.'

Kai said nothing for a moment but studied the painting with an expert eye. 'She is lovely,' he said musingly, and looked at Kate with one dark brow raised. 'And she *is* my cousin, Kate honey, even though it's only by adoption.'

'I didn't say she wasn't,' Kate assured him hastily, and sounded a little breathless.

The shrill call of the telephone possibly saved her from being reminded that her comments to Calvin about Iolani had almost caused a battle to evict Kai from the beach house, but he raised an expressive brow as he went to answer the phone.

Content to browse, Kate went through the remaining pictures stacked against the walls while Kai's voice reached her only faintly from the outer room. One or two she put aside as likely choices and it was while she was placing them beside an easel that she spotted two smaller canvases tucked away behind a box in the corner. Curious, she leaned across and picked them up.

The scene depicted was at once familiar and it took her only a second to realise why. It was the same pool she had found on her solitary walk along the cliffs—the crowding blossom trees and the falling water from the rocks, with the cool green water of the pool itself captured so exactly that she could almost feel its blessed coolness as she looked at it.

But it was not the scenery that held her gaze, but the single figure that appeared in both paintings. There was something all too familiar about the naked torso that emerged, waist-high, from the pool, arms raised to the falling water, brown hair spilling down over pale golden shoulders. She stared for a second in breathless disbelief, then her heart began hammering at her breast like a wild thing that sought to escape, and she felt a bright flush of colour in her cheeks.

She had believed herself unobserved when she took that impulsive dip in the cliff pool, now she knew there was a reason for that chittering bird who had protested so insistently among the blossom trees. The paintings were beautiful, she had to recognise that, but the sight of her own nakedness poised like some pagan naiad below the waterfall was both unexpected and disturbing.

'Kate?'

He came across the room towards her, soft-footed, his dark eyes unfathomable, and he took the paintings from her with firm but gentle hands, laying them down on a table before he turned back to her.

Kate, her heart still pounding crazily, stared at them still, her head shaking, a strange, blood-stirring sense of occasion curling her hands tightly. 'How could you?' she whispered at last. 'How could you, Kai? To——'

'Paint something so beautiful it took my breath away?' Kai interrupted softly. 'It was something I couldn't ignore when it was presented to me like a gift from heaven, Kate. You were never meant to see them.'

Kate could not look at him yet, she simply stood with her hands tight curled and her eyes on those symbols of her own recklessness, moved despite her reaction, by the sheer beauty of the whole scene. If she had looked at them and not recognised herself, she would have chosen them for the exhibition without hesitation.

'You won't——' She looked at him at last her eyes uncertain but appealing. 'You won't show them, Kai?'

He took her hands, his strong fingers squeezing hers tightly as if in reassurance, his voice soft, quiet and persuasive. 'Not if you forbid me to, my darling,' he said softly. 'They weren't meant for anyone but me.'

The endearment fell so easily from his lips and had such a wild and exciting effect on her senses that she looked up at him again, as if she had no option. His eyes glistened with some expression she did not remember seeing there before and she felt the sudden lurch her heart gave when she was pulled close into his arms again, her hands flat palmed against that broad golden chest.

'Kai——' Having said his name, she could not think clearly enough to say anything else, and he drew her to him, his mouth brushing gently on her forehead.

'You won't believe me if I say I love you, will you?' he asked, and Kate stirred against him, only too anxious to believe him, but not altogether trusting either her own emotions or his.

'Kai, I know you——'

'You don't, my love,' he argued, 'but that's something I propose doing something about in the very near future!'

'If you——'

Again he interrupted her, his mouth gently persuasive, then suddenly so fierce that she was swept along with a passion she made no attempt to resist. Her body bent like a willow in the wind, bowed by the irresistible pressure of his arms binding her to him.

His hands and the strong inescapable excitement of his body made nonsense of any thought of resistence, even if it had occurred to her, and she simply clung to him, uncaring about anything but being there with him.

She had sought him instinctively when she

needed comfort, but only in her innermost heart had she realised how much more he meant to her than a mere comforter. His mouth brushed her neck, sensually tender, pressed to the small throbbing pulse at the base of her throat, and his voice was muffled in the riot of nut-brown hair that tumbled about her shoulders.

'Did you really think I'd let you go to Cal Morton?' he whispered against her soft skin, and Kate sighed, her lips seeking the strong line of his jaw.

'I never meant to go to him,' she argued, and he eased her away from him for a moment, cradling her head in one big hand while the other still held her firmly against him.

'Never?' he asked, but gave her no time to answer.

Later, when she lay in his arms, tracing the outline of that wide and slightly lopsided mouth with one finger, he looked down at her with glittering eyes. 'Marry me, Kate,' he said huskily. 'I love you so much, and if you turn me down——' He shook his head and the lean hardness of his body was crushing in its urgency. 'I can't face the rest of my life without you, the way old Charlie had to without his Lizzie,' he whispered hoarsely, and Kate raised his head, her two hands either side of that dark, primitive face, gazing at it with soft, shining green eyes.

'You won't have to, Kai darling,' she promised, and with a soft, wordless cry he drew her again to his heart.

Romance
is
Beautiful

Get to the
HEART OF
HARLEQUIN

HARLEQUIN READER SERVICE is your passport to The Heart of Harlequin . . .

if You...

♥ enjoy the mystery and adventure that comes from the world's leading publisher of romantic novels . . .

♥ want to keep up-to-date on all of our new releases, eight brand new Romances and four Harlequin Presents, each month . . .

♥ are interested in valuable reissues of best-selling back titles . . .

♥ are intrigued by exciting, money-saving jumbo volumes . . .

♥ would like to enjoy North America's unique monthly magazine, "Harlequin" — available **ONLY** through Harlequin Reader Service . . .

♥ are excited by **anything new** under the Harlequin sun.

then...

YOU should be on the Harlequin Reader Service **INFORMATION PLEASE** list — it costs you nothing to receive our news bulletins and intriguing brochures. Please turn page for news of an **EXCITING FREE OFFER.**

a Special Offer for <u>You</u>...

Just by requesting information on Harlequin Reader Service, you will receive (with absolutely no obligation) an exciting and distinctively designed "limited-edition" copy of **Violet Winspear's** first Harlequin best seller

LUCIFER'S ANGEL

You will be fascinated with this explosive story of the fast-moving, hard-living world of Hollywood in the '50s. An unforgettable tale of an innocent young girl who meets and marries a dynamic but ruthless movie producer, this gripping novel combines excitement, intrigue, mystery and romance.

A complimentary copy is waiting for YOU — just fill out the coupon on the next page and send it to us today.